"Mr. Stillman
day," Alex c
have a lot of clothes to try on."

"Coming." Jack stepped out of the fitting room, adopting an innocent expression.

At the sound of the door clicking open, Alex looked up...and the pen slipped out of her suddenly loose hand. At first glance she feared he was naked, then realized with no small amount of relief that he was covered by a minuscule amount of stretchy black fabric. Sexual awareness zipped through her.

At last she dragged her gaze from him and pretended to study her papers. "I...don't recall seeing that particular...garment...on the list."

"They were on the pile," he said, shrugging. "This modeling stuff is new to me. Am I supposed to turn around or something?"

Alex swallowed. *Perhaps if she didn't have to look him in the eye...* "That...would be fine."

He turned to stand with his back to her. The underwear left nothing to the imagination. "You can turn around now," she said, struggling for composure.

He didn't move, and she suddenly noticed that his breathing was as erratic as hers. He lifted a hand to scratch his temple. "Gee, boss, I don't think that's such a great idea right now."

Dear Reader,

Every woman has one in her background—that sexy bad boy who revved up her engine but wasn't exactly marriage material. Rough, tough and unconventional, complete with motorcycle and to-die-for looks, they were the stuff our dreams were made of...and gave our fathers nightmares!

Well, meet Jack Stillman, a bad boy you can fall in love with, heart and soul. He's a former star athlete floating through life minding his own business until he meets Alexandria Tremont, heiress to a retail store chain, who suddenly holds his future in her prim little hands. Will Jack change his roguish ways for the love of a woman? Settle back to laugh, cry and root for Jack and Alex as they discover that the things in life they rebel against most are the very things they need to be happy.

I'd love to hear from you. Write to me at P.O. Box 2395, Alpharetta, GA 30023 and let me know if I'm keeping you entertained. Please watch for my next book, *Too Hot To Sleep*, a Temptation Blaze title available in June 2000. And don't miss my Christmas 2000 Temptation novel featuring a spin-off character from *It Takes a Rebel*.

Thanks for supporting the wonderful world of romance—please tell a friend about the powerful love stories you find within the pages of Harlequin Temptation.

Much love and laughter,

Stephanie Bond

IT TAKES A REBEL
Stephanie Bond

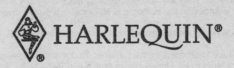

HARLEQUIN®

TORONTO • NEW YORK • LONDON
AMSTERDAM • PARIS • SYDNEY • HAMBURG
STOCKHOLM • ATHENS • TOKYO • MILAN • MADRID
PRAGUE • WARSAW • BUDAPEST • AUCKLAND

This book is dedicated to my editor, Brenda Chin,
who "gets it" and challenges me to be a better writer.

ISBN 0-373-25869-0

IT TAKES A REBEL

Copyright © 2000 by Stephanie Bond Hauck.

Visit us at www.romance.net

Printed in U.S.A.

1

"JACK, ARE YOU LISTENING?"

Jack Stillman jerked his attention back to his brother's voice on the phone. "Hmm? Sure, bro."

"I'm counting on you," Derek said in that patronizing big-brother tone that Jack hated.

He rolled his eyes, leaned back in his desk chair, and propped his feet on the corner of the desk. "Stop worrying, I can handle things until you get back."

"I'm not worried about your ability," Derek said dryly. "It's your dedication that keeps me up at night."

Jack frowned. "Your new bride should be the only thing keeping you up at night."

Derek chuckled in a way that told Jack he hadn't spent *every* minute of his honeymoon worrying about the ad agency. "Just remember—"

"I *know*, bro, I know. The gal from the IRS office will be by this afternoon, the phone bill needs to be paid, and I have an appointment with Al Tremont tomorrow morning at ten. I have everything under control."

"Since we need to make a good impression on this IRS agent, you might not want to call her 'gal.'"

He sighed, loath to spend the afternoon with some dried-up hag who wanted to scrutinize his W-4's.

"Is the office straightened up?" Derek asked.

Jack glanced at the pizza box sitting on his desk from yesterday, and the cartons of leftover Chinese from the day before. On the other side of the room that housed both his and Derek's desks, the floor-to-ceiling bookshelf had collapsed,

the timing of the mishap probably hastened by his overuse
of the mini-basketball hoop on the side, he conceded. Twice
he'd thought about straightening the mountain of reference
books and papers on the floor, then changed his mind. And
he hadn't gotten around to sorting the mail in the two weeks
since Derek had left. He raised the lid on the pizza box and
lifted the remaining stone-cold slice to his mouth for a bite.
"The place looks peachy," he said through a mouthful of
rubbery cheese.

"Good. Then tell me you dressed up."

Jack looked down at one of the short sleeve floral shirts
he'd acquired during his extended vacation in Florida, then
opened his top drawer and withdrew a black and white
striped tie from the wad of spares he kept there for emergencies. "Tie and everything," he said, flipping up the collar
of his shirt and fashioning a loose Windsor knot.

"And you got a haircut?"

He ran his hand through his dark shaggy hair and
grunted what he hoped passed for affirmation.

Derek sighed in relief, so he must have sounded convinc-
ing. "And you have ideas drawn up for Tremont?"

Jack shot a look in the direction of his sketch pad, then
flicked a chunk of pepperoni from the blank top sheet.
"Some of my best work ever."

"Great. What did you come up with?"

"Uh, I'll call you and go over the presentation when I get
everything back from the printer."

"You're the artist," Derek said with a little laugh. "I'm
nervous about you meeting with the IRS woman, but I have
to admit, I'm sure you'll do a good job with Tremont. This
account could put us in the big league, you know."

Jack winced and rubbed his stomach. Guilt and cold pizza
did not mix. "I know, Derek, I won't let you down." He
checked the clock on Derek's desk—he'd lost his own watch
in a poker game in Kissimmee—and straightened. The IRS
gal would arrive in another hour. "Listen, bro, gotta run."

"Call me on my cell phone if the agent has questions you can't answer."

"Sure thing. Give Janine a kiss for me, and make it French, okay?" He hung up before Derek could reprimand him, bit off another chunk of pizza, then winged it toward the overflowing trash can. After wiping his hands on his cut-off denim shorts, he pushed himself to his feet with an aggrieved sigh. Might as well get the darn bookshelf fixed.

He stretched tall into a mighty yawn, then padded barefoot to the closet they used as a supply room. He'd have time to slide into his deck shoes before the broad got there. Jack shook his head at the neat shelves, the bins of miscellaneous office supplies and the various tools. His brother had inherited their mother's penchant for order, while he had inherited their father's tendency toward turmoil.

God rest his father's sweet soul, the old man was still doing them favors. Paul Stillman, ever the generous spirit, had once stopped on New Circle Road to assist a motorist, only to discover the man was none other than Alexander Tremont, owner of the Tremont department store chain. Tremont had been on his way to a meeting at his flagship store in Lexington, Kentucky, and their father had given him a lift. When the two men hit it off, Tremont had promised the Stillman & Sons agency a chance at his business once his contract with a high-powered agency had run its course.

Last week, Al Tremont's secretary had phoned to keep his promise. Saddened to learn of their father's passing, Tremont nonetheless set an appointment to discuss ideas for a new ad campaign. Derek had been ecstatic when Jack told him, and considered cutting short his honeymoon, but Jack had assured him he could handle the presentation.

And he *could* handle the presentation, he told himself. He'd already performed some rudimentary research by calling acquaintances to ask what the hell the store sold. He still had nearly twenty-four hours until the Tremont appointment, and he always did his best work under pressure. If history repeated itself, his most creative ideas would strike him around three o'clock tomorrow morning.

He pulled down a tool belt and strapped it low around his hips. Begrudgingly, he lifted the stepladder to his shoulder—might as well change the two expired overhead lightbulbs while he was at it.

Upon closer inspection, the bookshelf was in worse shape than he'd thought. He ended up reinforcing the brace under each shelf and tightening every screw that held the piece together. Once the unit was stabilized, he positioned it against the wall, then knelt to start replacing the heap of books, binders and periodicals.

Two minutes into the pile, between volumes of advertising trade magazines, he stumbled across an old friend—the 1997 *Playboy* "Southern College Coeds" issue. A dog-eared page took him directly to the University of Kentucky offerings. Wow, still impressive. And by chance, he'd spotted the blonde in the cropped T-shirt at the next football game he'd attended. What was her name? Jack peered more closely. Oh, yeah—Sissy. He and Sissy had shared some good times.

"Excuse me."

At the sound of a woman's voice, Jack jerked his head up and slapped the magazine closed. In the doorway of their disheveled office stood the most drop-dead gorgeous woman he'd ever had the pleasure of setting his eyes upon. His body leapt in unadulterated admiration. The woman was...tight. Tight black hair bound away from her face. Tight skin over sharp cheekbones and a perfect nose. Tight set of her mouth and chin. Tight tailored pale blue suit that hugged every curve of her long body. Tight look from her haughty blue eyes. Tight grip on the black briefcase she held.

To say the IRS rep didn't look anything like what he'd expected was an understatement of laughable proportions. "Yes?" He adopted a charming expression. His mind raced ahead to the drinks, the dinner, the bed they were destined to share.

"I'm looking for Mr. Stillman."

Oh, and a husky voice, too. He'd surely died and gone to heaven. "You found him," he said, then tossed the magazine to the floor and walked toward her.

"You're Derek Stillman?" she asked, not hiding her surprise.

"No, I'm his brother, Jack, the better looking one." He grinned. "Derek is out of town, but I've been expecting you."

"Oh?" she asked, scanning the contents of the office. "You know who I am?"

"Sure," he said cheerfully. "Derek and I were just discussing the meeting on the phone."

Suddenly he realized the unkempt appearance of their office might run in their favor—the woman could certainly see they weren't hiding income. He laughed and gestured around. "As you can see, we're not exactly the cream of the advertising agencies." He made a rueful noise. "A month ago we were on the verge of bankruptcy, and now we're just hanging on by the skin of our ass—um, teeth, so this shouldn't take long."

"Indeed," she said, her enunciation clipped. "I believe I've seen enough." She turned as if to leave.

He panicked. "Wait—what about our appointment?"

"Consider it canceled."

Jack nearly whooped with relief—Derek would be ecstatic that the audit had been dismissed, but he wasn't about to let this creature just walk out of his life.

"You don't have to be so hasty," he drawled, strolling closer. "There's a silver lining to every cloud." When she turned back, he angled his head at her and gave her his most devilish grin. "How about dinner?"

One thin jet eyebrow shot up. "With you?"

He winked. "I grill a mean steak."

Her smile was, of course, tight. "I'm a vegetarian."

Jack blanched. He'd heard of vegetarians, but he'd never met one. "Well, I grill a mean...head of cabbage. What do you say?"

Her eyes narrowed. "I say 'no.' Goodbye, Mr. Stillman."

"Wait," he said, trotting after her into the reception area, where they kept a desk, a phone and an extinct computer for appearances. The two weeks' worth of mail nearly obscured the top of the dummy desk.

She turned again, her mouth pursed, her gaze chilly.

He spread his hands. "At least give me your card so I can prove to my brother that you were here." He'd call her and eventually wear her down—he always did.

The black-haired beauty hesitated, then withdrew a gold business card holder, extracted a card, and flicked it down on the corner of the reception desk. She opened the door and exited to the hall. Jack caught the door and stuck out his head to watch her walk away. Head up, her stride was long, and she never looked back as she disappeared around the corner.

Jack whistled low and under his breath. "Tight little behind, too." Spirits high, he turned back to the door and laughed aloud. The Stillman & Sons Advertising Agency sign on the outside of the door dangled crookedly by a thin chain. He'd been meaning to fix that, too, but the disrepair had undoubtedly been a bonus. He couldn't wait to call Derek, and he couldn't wait to call the mystery woman. He loved a gal who played hard to get.

Jack lifted his arm and patted himself heartily on the back. Derek was always complaining that he didn't pull his weight around the office, but from what he could see, running the place was a pure cinch. The auditor was practically in his pocket; in fact—he cracked his knuckles with one sweeping motion—maybe he'd be able to negotiate some sort of tax-free status between the sheets. He grinned— when he was hot, he was red-hot. Closing his eyes, he could practically feel the imprint of Tremont's handshake tomorrow as they agreed on a deal even more lucrative than his brother could have imagined. Humming in anticipation, Jack walked back into the messy reception area and picked up the card the smoky siren had left.

Then he nearly swallowed his smooth tongue.

Alexandria Tremont, Director of Marketing & Sales, Tremont Enterprises.

WHEN ALEX REACHED the parking lot, she was still marveling over the sheer audacity of Jack Stillman. She swung into her sedan, banged the door closed, and scoffed as she turned over the key in the ignition. The man was a joke, and a lame one at that. She wheeled out of the parking lot that was as shoddy as the so-called professional office buildings around it, making a wild guess as to the owner of the dusty black motorcycle sitting at a cocky angle.

She hesitated for half a heartbeat, tempted to lower the rag top of her white convertible on this sunny fall day, then decided she didn't want to have to bother with redoing her hair when she returned to the office. Funny, but she hadn't driven with the top down nearly as much as she thought she might when she'd bought the car on impulse last spring. Lately she'd been regretting her splurge; what had once sounded fun now seemed rather silly.

Alex dodged a pothole, then eased into side street traffic and headed for the bypass, her foot depressing the gas a little harder as the image of Jack Stillman's smug face rose in her mind. The nerve of the man, making a pass at her! Her cheeks warmed at the memory of his raking gaze, as if he were entitled or something, the cad.

The bronzed bum hadn't even bothered to put his best foot forward—or even don shoes for that matter—to impress a potentially huge customer. If there was one thing she resented, it was a man with an attitude who had absolutely nothing to back it up, and Jack Stillman appeared to be the

poster boy for arrogance. He'd obviously mistaken her for
the kind of woman who would be swayed by his stray-dog
good looks. The scoundrel undoubtedly planned to
shmooze her and her father with good-old-boy charm—a
southern staple she'd come to despise during her rise
through the ranks of the family business.

Her father had insisted, and rightfully so, that she start on
the sales floor as a teenager and learn the business from the
bottom up. Over the past fifteen years, she'd worked doubly
hard to overcome the stigma of being the boss's daughter.
Even her own father had resisted moving her into management, even though she knew the business inside out by the
time most kids were finishing college. She'd reached the
level of director two years ago, and was now in the running
for the position of vice president of sales and marketing recently vacated by a retiree. The competition was stiff, but
her record had been exemplary, and the new vice president
would be announced any day. Her father would be so
proud if the board of directors chose her.

Then, perhaps, Al would be forced to recognize her contribution to the company, to stop interfering with her duties
and decisions. This situation with the Stillman & Sons
agency was a perfect example. The vice presidential duties
had been split among the four sales directors for the time being, and though the responsibility of choosing a new advertising agency had been assigned to her, her father seemed
determined to give their considerable business to the doubt-
ful Stillman & Sons agency because of a from-the-hip promise he'd made to a Good Samaritan. The man had since
passed away, but Al wouldn't hear of 'going back on his
word.'

And now they were left to deal with a derelict son who
read *Playboy* at the office and fancied himself a ladies' man.
Alex sighed. She really didn't need the hassle.

She lifted the lid to a compartment on her armrest, removed her cellular phone, and punched in the number for her father's private line.

Her father answered after a half ring. "This is Al," he barked.

"It's Alex," she said. "Is this a bad time?"

"Never for you, Alex," he murmured, his voice softening. Despite his flaws, she really loved him. "What's up, my dear?"

"I just left the Stillman & Sons advertising agency."

"I thought the agency was sending someone here tomorrow morning."

The questioning tone in her father's voice made her squirm. "I, um, had some time and decided to pay them a courtesy visit."

"And?"

There it was again—that tone. "And they're not in our league, Dad." She winced at her slip because she preferred not to address him personally when they discussed business.

"What makes you say that?"

"The place is a mess, and Jack Stillman wasn't much better—raggedy, unclean, the man even asked me out." As if she would even *consider* going out with the buffoon.

"Can't fault his taste."

She rolled her eyes at his chuckle. "Stillman & Sons is a low-class operation."

"Did you see their portfolio?"

Alex balked. "It hardly seemed worth the trouble."

"Well, I have it on good faith that the agency is small, but good. I want to see what they have to offer. You're forgetting, Alex, *we* used to be the underdog."

Alex bit back her argument, knowing she couldn't change his mind when he was in such a mood. In fact, she was starting to worry that the reason she'd been chosen for this assignment was so her father could pull the strings without appearing to. "Okay," she conceded. "The appointment stands. I'll see you at ten in the morning."

"Have a nice day, sweetheart. By the way, Gloria wants you to come over for dinner soon."

She wrinkled her nose at the mention of her father's wife—the woman was dim *and* dull—then mouthed some vague response before saying goodbye. Alex disconnected the call, feeling torn, as usual, after talking to her father. Was it so wrong to want his love *and* his respect?

But as she replaced the phone, she suddenly realized she didn't have a thing to worry about where the meeting was concerned. Jack Stillman would swagger in tomorrow looking like a wasted tourist and even her honor-bound father would recognize the absurdity of working with the down-and-out agency.

Alex smiled and lifted her chin. With Jack Stillman's unwitting 'help' tomorrow morning, she'd be able to kill two birds with one stone: Her father would be forced to consider the reputable St. Louis advertising firm she was advocating, which also meant he would be forced to admit that she was right. And since the episode would unfold in the presence of various VIP's, her chance for the vice presidency would undoubtedly improve.

With a new outlook, she laughed aloud, mentally thanking the disreputable-looking advertising man for being in the wrong place at the right time. Her dear mother had once said that every event in this seemingly disjointed world actually happened for a reason. Apparently her mother's theory even extended to her unpleasant encounter with the repulsive Jack Stillman.

2

"DEREK'S GOING TO KILL ME." Jack held his head in his hands, fighting some kind of weird swirling sensation in his stomach. And his heart was racing as if he'd just run for a ninety-nine-yard touchdown. "He's absolutely going to kill me."

"In that case, I hope you have cash."

He glanced up to the open doorway. A plump fiftyish black woman stood dressed in white pants and shirt, wearing a lopsided red paper hat that read "Tony's." "You the stromboli sandwich with extra cheese?" she asked, her hand on one hip.

Jack nodded miserably, thinking even food wouldn't help his mood today.

"That'll be six dollars and forty cents." She dropped the sack on the desk unceremoniously and wiggled her fingers in his direction. Her fingernails were at least two inches long. And bright yellow.

With a heavy sigh, he pushed himself to his feet and removed his wallet. He counted eight one dollar bills into her hand, then added another when she lifted a winged eyebrow.

"You the handyman around here?" She nodded toward his tool belt as she stuffed the money into a fanny pack around her waist.

"Sort of," he mumbled. "This is my company...and my brother's."

"The murderer?"

Jack frowned. "Hmm?"

Her head jutted forward. "The man who's going to kill you—is he your brother?"

"Oh. Yeah."

"Why?"

"Why what?"

Her eyes rolled upward, and she spoke as if to a child. "Why is he going to kill you?"

Irritated by the woman's nosiness, he scowled. "It's a long story."

"Lucky for you," she said, revealing remarkably white teeth and surprising dimples. "You're my last delivery."

She had a pleasant way about her, he conceded, kind of...motherly. The woman was only trying to be nice, and what could it hurt to unload on a stranger? He shrugged, indifferent to her interest. "I'm supposed to be running this place while my brother is gone, but I f—" He swallowed at the disapproving look the woman shot him. "I mean, I messed up royally."

"How's that?"

He quirked his mouth from side to side. "A woman IRS agent was supposed to stop by, so when this gal showed up a while ago, I assumed she was here for the review."

"And?"

"And instead she was here about a huge account I'm supposed to pitch tomorrow—Tremont's department stores."

"And?"

"*And*, let's just say I downplayed the success of the business a tad—not the impression I was aiming for."

"So, who was she?" She leaned against the desk and studied her nails, obviously unaware of the significance of doing business with the southern retail chain.

"Alexandria Tremont. She must be related to the man who owns the place—"

"Daughter."

Jack stopped. "You know her?"

The woman ran a finger along the desk, then blew a quarter-inch of accumulated dust into the air. "I know *of* her. My son works in menswear at their store on Webster Avenue. Says that Tremont miss is a real go-getter."

"More like a real ball buster," he muttered to himself.

"Uh-huh, and not too bad to look at, if I recall."

"A little too skinny, if you ask me."

"And single, I think my boy said."

"No wonder—she's as cold as a freaking statue."

Her eyes didn't miss a thing, bouncing from an unturned calendar to a lopsided lamp shade to the silent computer. "Uh-huh. She's rich, too, I'll bet, and re-f-i-i-i-ned, with a royal shine."

He smirked, remembering that on top of everything else, Princess Tremont had caught him ogling a naughty magazine. "Well, she wasn't *that* impressive."

She glanced at his bare feet and lifted a long yellow nail. "As opposed to you?"

Jack frowned. "I don't make a habit of trying to impress people."

The woman crossed her arms over her matronly bosom. "You married?"

"No."

"Now there's a surprise."

"But my brother is," he added, as if Derek's goodness could atone for his own sins. "In fact, he's away on his honeymoon."

She sniffed. "When's he due back, your brother?"

"In another two weeks." Jack rubbed his temples as he picked up his earlier train of thought. "And Derek will kill me when he hears I've bungled this opportunity with Tremont."

The woman leaned over and walked her fingers through the mail pile, then harrumphed. "First, he'd have to find you in all this mess. Where's your office manager?"

"We don't have one."

"I'll take it," she said matter-of-factly, plucking her paper hat from her head and dropping it into the trash can.

Jack blinked. "Take what?"

"The job," she said, her voice indignant. "You get back to whatever it was you were fixing—I hope it was the sign on the door—and I'll get things organized in here."

"But there isn't a position—" The phone rang, cutting him off.

The woman yanked it up. "Stillman and Sons, how can I help you?"

She had spunk, he conceded. And a decent telephone voice.

"The overdue invoice for Lamberly Printing?"

She glanced at him, and he shook his head in a definite "no." The company simply didn't have the money.

"A check will be cut this afternoon," she sang.

Incredulous, Jack could only stare when she hung up the phone. Then he spat out, "We can't afford to pay that invoice!"

"I said a check will be cut, I didn't say for how much."

Jack pursed his mouth—not bad.

She picked up the greasy bag of food and shoved it into his hand. "Looks like you're having a working lunch." Dismissing him, she turned back to the mound of mail and began to toss junk letters into the trash.

He gaped. "Wait a minute. Who the devil *are* you?"

Without glancing up, she said, "Tuesday Humphrey, your new office manager."

He wondered if the woman was unstable, but her eyes were intelligent, and her hands efficient. Exasperated, Jack lifted his arms. "But we're not hiring an office manager!"

"I know," she said calmly. "Because the position has been filled."

The phone rang again, and she snapped it up. "Stillman

and Sons, how can I help you?" Her voice smiled. "Mr. Stillman is in a client meeting, but just a moment, and I'll check." She covered the mouthpiece. "Alexandria Tremont's secretary confirming your appointment at the Tremont headquarters at ten in the morning."

Jack squinted. "But she just *canceled* the appointment."

Tuesday uncovered the mouthpiece. "It was Mr. Stillman's understanding that the appointment was canceled. No? Hold, please, while I see if his schedule will still allow him to attend."

She covered the phone. "It's back on—are you in?"

He nodded, his shoulders sagging in relief.

Tuesday uncovered the mouthpiece. "Yes, ma'am, please tell Ms. Tremont that Mr. Stillman is looking forward to a productive meeting. Thank you for calling." She hung up the phone and returned to her sorting task. "Guess you still have a chance to impress the Tremonts."

"Guess so," he said, his mind racing.

"Well, get moving." She snapped her fingers twice. "We both have a heap of work to do."

Jack hesitated. "An IRS agent is supposed to come by."

"You already told me, remember?" She flung a water sports equipment catalogue into the trash.

His hand shot out in a futile attempt to retrieve the catalogue—he could use a new water ski vest. But at the challenging expression on Tuesday's face, he emitted a resigned sigh. The crazy woman couldn't do more damage to their business or reputation than he had. They had no money to steal, no trade secrets to pilfer, no client list to filch. And at least he wouldn't have to answer the damn phone. "Knock yourself out," he said, splaying his hands. "But I can't pay you."

He stepped into the hall and closed the front door behind him to tackle the lopsided sign first. Within a few moments he'd rehung the smooth plaque of walnut upon which their father had painstakingly lettered and gilded the words "Stillman & Sons Advertising Agency" nearly twenty-five years ago. Without warning, grief billowed in his chest as his father's easy grin rose in his mind.

At his wife's encouragement, Paul Stillman had abandoned his modest home studio to become an entrepreneur when the boys were pre-teens. Jack had viewed the move as an act of treason against his father's natural calling. He'd admired his father's independence, his ability to adequately, if not luxuriously, provide for the family with the lively paintings he sold to local designers and businesses. He hadn't wanted to see his father saddled with overhead and commuting and sixty-hour work weeks, but his father said the earning potential was better, and he owed their mother a retirement fund.

Indeed, his father had set aside a nice nest egg doing graphic artwork and ad plans for small- to medium-size businesses in Lexington, and later, mail order catalogs. Stillman & Sons had been a true family business—their mother ran the office, Derek had cut his accounting teeth on the books. Even Jack had pitched in on occasion, brainstorming with his father on the more creative projects, although the business itself had held—and still held—an unpleasant association for him. He banged down the hammer, connecting with his thumb instead of the nail head, then cursed and sucked away some of the pain.

He'd watched the stress of the agency take its toll on his otherwise carefree father. His hair had seemed to gray overnight, and worry lines had plowed deep into his forehead. His paintbrush and easel had languished, and little by little, Paul Stillman's zest for root beer and whistling and people-watching had drained away.

Oh, his father had remained easygoing enough, but his good cheer seemed forced, and he'd stopped visiting the local art galleries, once a favorite getaway for him and his younger, more creative son. Jack missed those outings and he blamed the family business for taking his father away from him. At thirty-four, he recognized those feelings as childish, but he stubbornly clung to them nonetheless. From his perspective, responsibility sucked the life out of a man and left him with less to offer the very people he was trying to provide for.

Jack pulled a bandanna handkerchief from his back pocket and slowly wiped dust from the plaque. Frowning wryly, he scrubbed especially hard on the ending *s* in "Sons," half hoping the letter would disappear. If truth be known, Derek was the son who deserved the agency—Jack wasn't sure why his brother vehemently insisted he remain a partner.

Predictably, Derek had joined the agency full time when he graduated college, and the family expected nothing less of Jack. Instead, two years later he'd skipped his own graduation ceremony and hitchhiked to New Orleans where he'd put his two degrees—art and international business— to use by becoming the premiere artisan in Blue Willie's infamous tattoo parlor just off Bourbon Street. By some stroke of divine luck, Jack had decided to return to Kentucky two years ago only weeks before a heart attack had claimed his father.

And except for a few "sabbaticals" here and there, he'd remained in Kentucky to help Derek run the agency, which had lapsed into a slow decline after their father had died. Their mother had turned to traveling with her sister, and Derek...well, Derek had turned into a tyrant—although, Jack conceded, he himself hadn't been the model business partner. An unpleasant feeling ballooned in his chest, but he'd always refused to waste time on useless emotions like guilt, remorse, love, or hate. Funny, but all kinds of strange sensations seemed to be rolling around in his empty stomach this morning. It was as if Alexandria Tremont had set the tone for the day. Jack kneaded the tight spot just below his breastbone. The sooner he ate that sandwich, the better.

Swinging open the door, he was startled by a cheerful humming sound. He'd nearly forgotten about the self-proclaimed new office manager. Poor lady—she was probably bored and neglected by her son, looking for some way to kill time. Wonder what Derek would say?

Oh, what the hell, Derek had left *him* in charge, hadn't he?

To her credit, Tuesday had performed small miracles in the few minutes he'd been in the hallway—the mail lay in three neat piles, and the desk and bookshelves fairly gleamed. She had found a radio and tuned in a local light-rock station, which provided the background for her spirited humming.

"Two phone messages," she said, handing him pink slips of paper. "Bill collectors, both of them. I told them our accounting staff was preparing for an audit, and bought you a few days."

Jack grinned. "Great."

"Just a few days," she warned, as she moved around the room, cleaning with what he recognized as his favorite tie-dyed T-shirt, which he'd been looking for. She stopped long enough to shake her finger at him. "So you'd better not blow that meeting tomorrow, young man."

Properly chastised by a virtual stranger, he lifted his hands and escaped into the back office to finish the bookshelf. He tested the unit's sturdiness and methodically replaced the books, but his mind wasn't on the task at hand.

Jack simply couldn't shake the memory of Alexandria Tremont standing there appraising him with her cool, disapproving eyes, her nose conveniently tweaked upward by nature to spare her the trouble of having to lift it when she spoke. He'd seen that look before, the sneer that branded him a loser by people who didn't know that he could have been a hotshot executive had he simply chosen to be. At the meeting tomorrow he'd just have to show the uppity woman that he could hold his own among her kind.

Then he was angry at himself for wanting to impress anyone, much less Alexandria Tremont. He smoothed his ruffled pride by reasoning he was doing it for Derek and for the good of the agency, but anger fueled his energy. By the time he'd returned the books to the shelves and replaced the two lightbulbs, Jack felt that strange prickly feeling again, that alien sensation.

Apprehension? Jack inhaled deeply, but the tightness in his chest didn't diminish. Could be. Derek had certainly complained enough about being apprehensive over one thing or another—perhaps this roiling nausea was why his brother kept a bottle of Pepto-Bismol in his desk and in the glove compartment of his ultraconservative car.

Jack stooped to retrieve a can of beer from his desk drawer, but froze when he heard raised voices from the front office. The IRS agent? He slipped into his shoes, removed the tool belt, and jogged to the front, but his feet faltered when he saw that Tuesday had a suited man pinned facedown on the desk, one arm behind him. The man's face was a mask of pain.

"Tuesday!" Jack bellowed. "What the devil are you doing?" He reached for her hands and pried them loose from the visitor's arm, despite her protests.

"I'm trying to help the poor man," she insisted, resisting Jack. "He said his back was hurting, so I gave him an adjustment."

"This maniac popped a bone in my neck," the red-faced man yelped. "She probably crippled me!"

When at last he righted the man to a seated position, Jack shoved his hands on his hips and glared at Tuesday while introducing himself to the stranger. "I'm Jack Stillman, and I apologize, Mr.—?"

"Stripling," the smallish man chirped, straightening his tie. "Marion Stripling, IRS."

Jack closed his eyes. *Marion*—no wonder Derek had told him to expect a female. "I apologize, Mr. Stripling, for this woman's—" he shot her a lethal look "—complete lapse in judgment. Truthfully, I don't even know her myself."

The man looked incredulous. "What, did she just wander in off the street?"

"Something like that," Jack mumbled.

"What kind of a loony bin operation are you running here?"

"One that's losing money," Jack assured him. "Mr. Stripling, this way back to my desk, please. I need to have a word with my *office manager.*"

The man scowled in Tuesday's direction, then picked up his briefcase and fled in the direction Jack indicated.

Jack turned back to Tuesday. "Well?"

She maintained a haughty position. "My late husband was a chiropractor. When Mr. Stripling told me he'd been delayed because of back pain, I was simply trying to help."

His eyes widened. "By holding him down against his will and popping a bone in his neck?"

She wagged a finger in the air, her hip cocked to one side. "You'll see, he'll be thanking me."

"*You'll* see, he'll be *suing* me!" Jack sputtered, then held his temples, at a loss what to do next.

The phone rang, and she jerked it up. "Stillman and Sons, Lexington's number one advertising agency. How can I help you? Yes, hold please." She covered the mouthpiece, then smiled sweetly and held the phone in Jack's direction. "It's your brother."

3

ALEX STRETCHED HIGH to relieve the pressure of bending over the desk in her apartment for the past hour, then reached for the crystal goblet of white wine she'd been nursing since arriving home from her typical twelve-hour day. Using her stockinged foot, she levered the chair around to stare over the lights of downtown Lexington. It was another in a string of unusually warm October evenings. On impulse, she'd opened the sliding glass door leading to her balcony to dilute the stale air in her condo. The fresh breeze and the view revived her.

The University of Kentucky was having some kind of sports function because the streets leading to campus were choked. Not particularly fond of sports, she nonetheless recognized the huge economic advantage of having a popular college athletic program in town: athletics attracted attention for the university, swelling the student population, and college students remained the strongest buying group for the local Tremont department stores.

Alex swallowed a mouthful of chardonnay, thinking she should attend a college game of some sort with her father, a bona fide sports nut, just to see what all the fuss was about. On the other hand, Heath would undoubtedly take her in grand style if she wanted to go, even though he wasn't much of a sports buff either.

Heath Reddinger had been scrupulously accommodating to both her and her father since joining the senior management of Tremont's as Chief Financial Officer. She had liked him immediately—he was handsome, intelligent and sensitive. Her father, on the other hand, had never taken to Heath, although Al appreciated his contribution to the company, and had nodded in acquiescence when she and Heath had become engaged two months ago. Alex smiled as she fingered the diamond solitaire he'd given her. Heath was hard-working, predictable and fairly low-maintenance. She appreciated men with nice, neat edges.

Her smile faded when the face of Jack Stillman appeared to taunt her. The unkempt man was a loose cannon. She knew instinctively he was just the kind of man who could stir her father to rebellion. But she was determined to work with the St. Louis ad firm who could put Tremont's on the same page as Roark's and Tofelson's—two southeastern chains with toeholds in Louisville which, according to a survey she'd commissioned in her position as Director of Marketing and Sales, were ranked higher than Tremont's in perception of quality and style. In layman's terms, the other stores were deemed more classy than Tremont's. But the St. Louis ad agency could change all that. Just last year, they'd taken an unknown soft drink into the sales stratosphere with an award-winning campaign.

Her phone rang, rousing her. Heath's name appeared on the caller ID screen, so she picked up the cordless extension, along with her goblet of wine and headed toward the kitchen. "Hello."

"Hi, honey."

She stopped to straighten a pillow on the sofa—living in an open loft apartment meant everything had to be in its place. "Hi. Did you get my message?"

"Yes. Do you want me to come over?"

They hadn't slept together in weeks, but she simply wasn't up to his lengthy, methodical foreplay rituals tonight, not with work issues weighing on her mind. "I'm really tired, and my day is packed tomorrow."

"Oh, okay." Agreeable, as always. "By the way, Al asked me to sit in on the morning meeting with the local ad agency. I hope that's okay with you."

She'd suspected as much—her father was gathering supporters, and he knew Heath was anxious to gain his favor. Alex pursed her mouth, weighing her response. "That's why I called, although I personally think the meeting will be a waste of time. I paid the agency a surprise visit today and the owner is a Neanderthal."

"Hmm. Did you tell your father?"

"Sure, but he insists on going through with this charade because of a promise he made to the former owner of the agency."

"Well." Heath hesitated, always a little nervous when she disagreed with her father. "I guess it'll be a short meeting."

"Uh-huh," she agreed as she moved into the tiny blue and chrome kitchen nook situated in a corner. "I'm sure you'll agree with me wholeheartedly once you meet this character." She recorked the wine bottle and returned it to a shelf in the refrigerator door. "We'll have to stick together to convince Daddy that we need to elevate the quality of the firms we do business with. You know—being judged by the company we keep, and all that jazz."

"Okay," he agreed, but he sounded as if he were sitting on a fence row, casting glances on either side.

She tore off a paper towel and wiped a ring of moisture gathered on the tile counter where the bottle had sat. "Maybe we can have dinner tomorrow night."

"Great! I'll make reservations at Gerrard's."

Her favorite—Heath was such a gentleman. For a few seconds, she reconsidered having him come over, then decided guiltily that she needed the sleep more than the physical attention. "Gerrard's sounds wonderful. I'll talk to you tomorrow."

After disconnecting the call, Alex removed the pins from

her hair and sighed, feeling restless and antsy for some reason she couldn't quite put her finger on. She grabbed a magazine and her half-full glass, then fell into her white overstuffed chair-and-a-half and propped her feet on the matching ottoman. With the pull of a delicate chain, she turned on a Tiffany-style floor lamp and fingered the large porcelain bead at the end of the chain, studying the intricate design she had memorized long ago.

The lamp had been a moving-in gift from her mother when Alex had first bought the spacious loft condo. She wasn't sure which one of them was more excited with the find, but then her mother had passed away suddenly, before they'd had a chance to decorate the unique space together. Alex knew it sounded corny, but when she sat under the lamp, she felt as if her mother's spirit glowed all around her. She sipped from her glass, and idly fingered the pages of the magazine, subconsciously absorbing the latest styles, colors and accessories. The store carried that line of coats...that line of separates...that line of belts.

Jack Stillman...Jack Stillman. Alex laid her head back and frowned at the antique tin ceiling she'd painted a luminous pewter. Why did his name tickle the back of her memory? Perhaps it was just one of those names...

A frenzied knock on her door interrupted her thoughts. She knew who it was even before she pushed herself to her feet and padded across the white wood floor, but she checked the peephole just in case. Lana Martina, friend, fool, and neighbor, peered back at her, her arched white eyebrows high and promising.

Alex's spirits lifted instantly—Lana was a full-fledged, flat-out, certified nut who just happened to have taken a liking to quiet, scholarly Alex while they were in high school. Within the halls of their private Catholic school, Lana was a walking scandal, her pleated skirt always a little too short, her polished nails always a little too long. But her incredible intellect had kept the nuns at bay. In fact, Alex had met her on the debate team, and while the girls couldn't have come from more different backgrounds, they had formed a lasting friendship.

Alex swung open the door, smiling when she saw Lana held two pint-sized cartons of ready-to-spread cake frosting. "Mocha cocoa with artificial flavoring?" her friend asked, reading from the labels. "Or fantasy fudge with lots of nasty preservatives?"

"Fantasy fudge," Alex said, standing aside to allow Lana in. Her friend was as slim as a mannequin, but her personality needed as much room as possible.

"I brought utensils," Lana said, holding up two silver dessert spoons. "It's such a pain to get chocolate out from under your fingernails."

Alex took the proffered spoon and carton of icing, then followed Lana to the sitting area. Having performed this ritual countless times, they assumed their respective corners of the comfy red couch, Alex's feet curled beneath her, Lana sitting cross-legged.

"Nice silver," Alex observed, studying the intricate pattern on the end of the heavy spoon.

"It belongs to Vile Vicki." Lana ripped the foil covering off the top of her carton.

"You *stole* her silver?"

"Borrowed," Lana corrected, dipping in her spoon and shoveling in a mound of chocolate big enough to choke two men. "She's such a witch," she said thickly.

Alex smiled, then spooned in a less impressive amount of the creamy fudge icing, allowing the sweet, chocolaty flavor to melt over her tongue before she responded. "She can't be that bad."

"You don't live with her," Lana insisted. "The woman is simply the most self-absorbed, tedious, annoying female I've ever met."

"There's Gloria the Gold Digger," Alex said, pointing her spoon.

"At least she was smart enough to marry your father."

"True," Alex conceded with a sigh. Hopes that she and her father would become closer after her mother died had been dashed by Gloria Bickum Georgeson Abrams. The woman had brought a disposable pan of the most hideous macaroni salad to their home after her mother's funeral, and had been underfoot ever since.

"I swear, Alex, I'm going to kill her."

"Gloria?"

"No, Vicki. Do you know what she did?"

"I can't guess."

"Guess."

"I can't."

"Sure you can."

Alex sighed. "Borrowed your suede coat again?"

"She *ruined* it. No, worse."

"Forgot to pay a bill?"

"I had to flash the cable man so he wouldn't cut us off. But it's worse."

"What?"

"Guess."

"Lana—"

"She's dating Bill Friar."

Alex swallowed. "Oh." Lana was the most popular, outgoing woman she knew, and her looks were extraordinary, if offbeat—classic bone structure and violet-colored eyes allowed her to pull off spiky bleach-white hair. But Lexington men did not stand in line for eccentric-looking women with an I.Q. that put her on the Mensa mailing list. Bill Friar had seemed to be the exception—at first. Then the big phony had broken her friend's big heart.

"Yeah, 'oh,' is right." Lana shoveled in another huge bite. "She has the nerve to rub it in my face."

Alex felt a pang for her friend. "Are they getting serious?"

"No, she's dating a dozen other guys. She only went out with him to get back at me."

"How did she know you and Bill were once an item?"

Lana stirred the spoon aimlessly, her eyebrows drawn together. "She read my diary."

Alex sucked on her spoon, her eyes wide. "She didn't."

"She did and, just watch, I'm going to get her back."

"Why don't you just find another roommate?"

"We both signed the lease, so I'm stuck for another eight months, but after that, I'm outta there. Meanwhile," Lana said, holding up the ornate spoon, "I'm going to borrow *her* things for a while. These are her earrings, too."

Alex leaned forward to get a better look at the copper spheres. "Nice."

"Aren't they? So what's new with you?" Lana asked, fully vented and ready to listen. "I phoned you this morning for lunch, but your secretary said you were out."

"I was running an errand on the east side."

"Eww. Why?"

Alex took another slow bite before answering. "Ever hear of a guy named Jack Stillman?"

Her friend blinked. "Sure. Hotshot receiver for UK when we were freshmen. Don't you remember?"

Alex worked her mouth from side to side. "Maybe, maybe not."

"Great looking, big man on campus, dated the varsity *and* the junior varsity cheerleading squads."

"He sounds pretty forgettable."

Lana laughed. "He had a perfect record his senior year— never once dropped the ball. Of course I'm not surprised you don't remember. You practically slept at the store back then to impress Daddy, not that things have changed much in fifteen years." Her smile was teasing. "You really need to get out more, Alex."

"Heath and I go out."

"That tree? *Please.* My blow up doll Harry is more exciting."

Alex had heard Lana's lukewarm opinion on Heath too many times to let the comment bother her. So he wasn't Mr. Excitement—she didn't mind. "To each her own."

Lana put away another glob of empty calories. "I suppose. Why the questions about Jack Stillman?"

"He owns an ad agency in town and he's pitching to us in the morning."

"Well, I guess he grew up after all."

"I wouldn't go that far," Alex said dryly. "This morning I dropped in to check out his operation and had the displeasure of meeting the man."

Lana leaned forward, poised for gossip. "Is he still gorgeous?"

"I couldn't tell under that heavy layer of male chauvinism."

Her friend frowned, then her mouth fell open. "He got under your skin, didn't he?"

Alex squirmed against the suddenly uncomfortable overstuffed goose down cushions. "Not in the way you're implying."

Lana whooped. "Oh, yeah, under like a syringe."

She sighed, exasperated. "Lana, believe me, the man is no one I would remotely want to work with."

"So, who's talking about work?"

Alex rolled her eyes. "Or anything else. He's a player if I've ever seen one, and the man doesn't exactly scream success, if you know what I mean."

Lana made a sympathetic sound. "Too bad. He used to be hot."

"I believe he still operates under that delusion."

"So you don't think he'll get your business?"

"Not if I can help it."

"Well, let me know how it goes," Lana said, standing and stretching into a yawn.

Alex frowned. "You have to go already?"

"Four-thirty comes mighty early."

"When are you going to buy that coffee shop?"

"Maybe when I acquire a taste for the dreadful stuff," her friend said with a grimace. "I still keep a stash of Earl Grey under the counter. I'm busy tomorrow, but let's have lunch the day after and you can let me know how it goes with Jack the Attack."

"Jack the Attack?"

Lana nodded toward the wall of bookshelves. "Check your college yearbook, bookworm. Goodnight."

"Here's your spoon."

Lana grinned. "Keep it."

Alex was still laughing when the door closed behind her friend, but sobered when Jack Stillman's face rose in her mind to taunt her. The man was shaping up to be more of a potential threat than she'd imagined. She walked over to a laden bookshelf and removed the yearbook for her freshman year of college. Within seconds, she located the sports section and, as Lana had said, it seemed that Jack Stillman had been the man of the hour. Although UK was renowned for all of its team sports programs, Jack the Attack had been heralded for single-handedly taking his football team to a prestigious post-season bowl game, and winning it.

Page after page showed Jack in various midmotion poses: catching the football, running past opponents, crossing into the end zone. The last page featured Jack in his mud-stained uniform, arm in arm with a casually dressed man who was a taller, wider version of himself, behind whose unsuspecting head Jack was holding up two fingers in the universal "jackass" symbol. Twenty-two-year-old

Jack had the same killer grin, the same mischievous eyes, with piles of dark, unruly hair in a hopelessly dated style. Alex smirked as she mentally compared the boy in the picture to the man she'd met this morning. Too bad he was such a cliché—a washed-up jock still chasing pom-poms.

Alex snapped the book closed. The ex-football star angle worried her. Her father was already aware of it, she was sure, and the fact that he hadn't taken the time to enlighten her probably meant he would bend over backward to work with Stillman just to be able to tell the guys at the club about the man's athletic accomplishments.

Anger burned the walls of her stomach, anger about the old boy's network, anger toward men who shirked their duties but advanced to high-ranking corporate positions because they had a low golf handicap and could sweat with male executives in the sauna. Subtle discrimination occurred within Tremont's, although she was working judiciously to address disparity within the sales and marketing division. And subtle discrimination occurred within her own family. Had she been a son, an athlete, she was certain her father would have showered her with attention, would have fostered her career more aggressively. She ached for the closeness that she'd once shared with her mother, but that seemed so out of reach with her father.

She blinked back tears, feeling very alone in the big, high-ceilinged apartment. Fatigue pulled at her shoulders, but the sugar she'd ingested pumped through her system. She needed sleep, but her bed, custom made of copper tubing and covered with a crisp white duvet, looked sterile and cold in the far corner of the rectangular-shaped loft.

Alex located her glass of wine and finished it while standing at the sink. Knowing the ritual of preparing for bed sometimes helped her insomnia, she moved toward the bedroom corner to undress. After draping the pale blue suit over a chrome valet, she dropped her matching underwear into a lacy laundry bag. From the back of her armoire, she withdrew a nappy, yellow cotton robe of her mother's and wrapped it around her. After removing her makeup with more vehemence than necessary, she walked past her bed and returned to the comfy chair she'd abandoned when Lana arrived, covering her legs with a lightweight afghan.

But she lay awake long after she'd extinguished her mother's light, straining with unexplainable loneliness and frustration, stewing over unjust conditions she might never be able to change. Right or wrong, she channeled her hostility toward the one person who, at the moment, best epitomized life's arbitrary inequities: Jack Stillman. Clodhopping his way through life and having the Tremont business laid at his feet because he was a man and a former sports celebrity simply wasn't fair.

Remembering Lana's words, Alex set her jaw in determination. Perfect record be damned. The infamous "Jack the Attack" Stillman had already dropped the ball—he just didn't know it yet.

4

"*DON'T DROP THE BALL, JACK.*"

Derek's words from much earlier in the workday reverberated in his head. In the middle of the crisis with the IRS guy, Jack had somehow explained away Tuesday's presence—later he'd given her a fifty dollar bill and told her not to come back—and he managed to convince Derek that he had everything under control, including the Tremont's presentation.

Jack swore, then tore yet another sheet from his newsprint drawing pad, wadded it into a ball, and tossed it over his shoulder with enough force to risk dislocating his elbow. His muse had truly abandoned him this time. Three-thirty in the morning, with no revelation in sight. Forget the printer—this presentation would have to consist of raw drawings and hand-lettering.

If he ever came up with an idea, that is.

"Think, man, think," he muttered, tapping his charcoal pencil on the end of the desk, conjuring up key words to spark his imagination. *Clothes, style, fashion, home decor.* He needed a catchy phrase to convince people to shop at Tremont's.

Shop till you drop at Tremont's spot.

If you got the money, honey, we got the goods.

Spend a lot of dough at Tremont's sto'.

Okay, so he was really rusty, but at least it was a start.

He sketched out a few unremarkable ideas, but a heavy stone of dread settled in his stomach—this was not the best stuff that had ever come out of his pencil. The tight little bow of Alexandria Tremont's disapproving mouth had dogged him all evening. The woman obviously didn't expect much and, despite his efforts to the contrary, that was exactly what he was going to deliver. Dammit, he hated wanting to impress her...not that it mattered now.

Pouring himself another cup of coffee from a battered thermos, he raked a hand over his stubbly face and leaned back in his chair. Jack winced as the strong, bitter brew hit his taste buds at the same time a bitter truth hit his gut: He was washed up. Being at the top of his game—no matter what the arena—used to come so easily, and now he was struggling for mere mediocrity.

His college football career had been a joyous four-year ride of accolades, trophies and popularity—a young man's dream that afforded him unbelievable perks, including as many beautiful women as he could handle, and enough good memories to last a lifetime. But for all his local celebrity and natural talent, he hadn't even considered going pro, partly because he didn't want to put his body through the paces, and partly because he'd simply wanted to do more with his life, to strike out and experience new settings, new people. And frankly, he'd always hated doing what was expected of him, whether it meant playing pro football or working for the family ad agency. Until now, he hadn't realized how much he missed striving for something beyond having enough beer to wash down the native food of wherever he happened to be.

But inexplicably, the yearning that had lodged in his stomach the previous day had permeated other vital organs until he could feel it, see it, breathe it—the need to achieve. The need to make something out of nothing. The need to prove to others that he could hack it in any environment. The need to prove to himself that he still had his edge. And, he admitted with the kind of brutal honesty that comes to a man in the wee hours of the morning, Alexandria Tremont played a startling role in his reawakening. Just the thought of the challenge in her ice-blue eyes brought long dormant feelings of aspiration zooming to the surface. He hadn't felt this alive since he was carried off the football field on the shoulders of his teammates for the last time. He wanted this win so badly, he could taste her—er, it.

The rush of adrenaline continued to feed his brain, which churned until the light of early dawn seeped through the windows. Jack discarded idea after idea, but he refused to give up hope that something fantastic would occur to him.

Around seven, and with little to show for his sleepless night, Jack heard a scratching sound on the front door. He went to investigate, stapler in hand for lack of a better weapon. To his abject consternation, Tuesday opened the door and marched inside, flipping on lights as she went. She wore an attractive flowered skirt and a modest blouse. "Morning," she sang.

"How'd you get in?" he demanded.

She held up a Tremont's department store credit card, of all things. "I jiggled the lock—this is no Fort Knox, sonny. You're here early."

"I didn't leave," he said, scowling. "And I thought I told you not to come back."

"You were having a bad day," she said cheerfully. "So I thought I'd give you another chance." She leaned toward him and grimaced. "Oooh, you don't look so good."

"I know."

"Did you finish the presentation?"

"Yes."

"Is it good?"

"No."

She sighed, a sorrowful noise. "Well, you'll have to wow them with charm, I suppose." She squinted, angling her head. "What were you planning to wear?"

He looked down at his disheveled beach clothes and shrugged. "I hadn't thought about it, but I'm sure I can rustle up a sport coat."

Tuesday grunted and picked up the phone. "What are you, about a forty-four long?"

He shrugged again, then nodded. "As best as I can remember."

She looked him up and down. "Six-three?"

Again, he nodded.

"Size twelve shoe?"

"Thirteen if I can get them. Why?"

Tuesday waved her hand in a shooing motion. "Go take a shower and shave that hairy face. Hurry, and yell for me when you're finished."

Jack wasn't sure if he was simply too tired to argue, or just glad to have someone tell him what to do. The Tremont's account was lost now anyway—he would merely go through the motions for Derek's sake.

He retreated to the bathroom in the back, grateful for the shower the landlord had thought to build. Shaving had never been a favorite chore, and it took some time to clear the dark scruff from his jaw. He checked in the cabinet on the wall, and sure enough, Derek had left a couple pairs of underwear, along with a pair of faded jeans and a few T-shirts. Derek was more thick-bodied than he, but the underwear would work. Jack had barely snapped the waistband in place when an impatient knock sounded at the door.

"You through in there?"

"Give me a second," he called, then wrapped a towel around his waist before opening the door.

Tuesday strode in, carrying a comb and a pair of scissors.

"Oh, no," Jack said, shaking his head. "You're *not* cutting my hair."

"Oh, yes," she said, motioning for him to sit on the commode lid. "That wooliness has to come off. Come on, now, don't argue."

He stubbornly crossed his arms and remained standing.

She pointed the scissors at him. "Don't make me climb up there. Do you want to blow this chance completely?"

Jack sighed and shook his head.

"Then sit."

He sat. And she cut. And cut and cut and cut.

Cringing at the mounds of dark hair accumulating on the floor around him, Jack pleaded, "Gee, at least leave me enough to comb."

She stepped back, made a few final snips, then nodded and whipped off the towel protecting his shoulders. "There, you look human again." Tuesday exited the bathroom with purpose.

Half afraid to look in the mirror, Jack did so one eye at a time. Damn. He pursed his mouth and lifted a hand to his sheared head. It was short, but it didn't look half bad. He turned sideways and ran a hand over the back of his neck. "Long time, no see," he murmured. He leaned over the sink and wet his short hair, then combed it back. "Hello, ears."

"Here you go, handsome."

Tuesday was back, this time holding a vinyl suit bag.

"Suit, shirt, cuff links, tie, socks, belt and shoes, size twelve—your toes'll be pinched just a mite."

Jack's eyes widened. "Where did you get this stuff?"

"My son, Reggie," she said. "Remember, he works for Tremont's?"

"Oh, right," he said. "Menswear?"

She nodded. "Natty dresser, my Reggie." She handed him the bag. "Clothes make the man, you know."

Touched, Jack reached for the bag, then stopped and stared at her. "Tuesday, you're a genius."

She gave him a dismissive wave. "I know that, son. What took you so long to catch on?"

Jack unzipped the bag, his mind jumping ahead to his blank sketch pad. He had about an hour to get a new idea down on paper.

"Tuesday, I'm going to be cutting it close. Will you call me a taxi?" A trip across town on his motorcycle might compromise the condition of his portfolio, he realized.

"I did. It'll be here at a quarter to ten," she said, then turned and closed the door.

Jack grinned at his own reflection, suddenly feeling young again. He was back, and good wasn't a big enough word to express how he felt. He felt...he felt...*energized*. And lucky. And teeming with fiery anticipation at the look on the ice princess's face when he walked through the door.

"Look out, Ms. Alexandria Tremont," he murmured. "Ready or not, here I come."

THE FAVORITE PART of Alex's day was walking through the various departments of Tremont's before the doors opened to the public. This morning, she acknowledged, the routine also served to soothe her anxiety about the impending advertising meeting. Actually, she felt a little sorry for Jack Stillman—the clueless man was in way over his swollen head. But regardless of her opinion of him and his agency, she honestly didn't enjoy watching people make fools of themselves. Alex sighed and sipped coffee from a stoneware mug. Hopefully the meeting would be mercifully short.

Her mood considerably lighter this morning than the previous evening, the store seemed exceptionally pleasing: the sweep of formal gowns on so-slim mannequins, the musky blend of popular perfumes, the neat stacks of thick towels on cherry tables, the flash of silver tea sets. In the past decade, Tremont's had made the subtle move from a discount department store to a more upscale shopping experience for the upper-middle class of Lexington and the surrounding area. Alex liked to believe her sales and marketing policies of pushing retail boundaries had something to do with the transformation.

She stopped to compliment Carla, one of the most senior salesclerks who always arrived at her station in the jewelry department early enough to give the glass counter an extra swipe, then Alex moved toward the stairs by way of menswear. A tall well-dressed youth was tagging slacks for alterations, his hands moving swiftly. Alex's mind raced as she tried to recall his name—she'd seen it at the top of the commission lists often enough. Ronnie? No, Reggie.

"Good morning, Reggie."

He jerked up his head and dropped the pants he held. "G-good morning, Ms. Tremont," he said as he hurriedly knelt to retrieve the clothes. "Sorry, I'm clumsy today."

Alex dipped to help him. "Nonsense." But she did squint at his dark head that was tilted down. She'd spoken to the young man several times and she'd never known him to be nervous, yet his hands were practically shaking. "Is everything all right, Reggie?"

"Hmm? Oh, yes, ma'am. Just fine." But he made only fleeting eye contact as he straightened.

"Good." Alex stood and brushed off the behavior with a smile, then rescued a navy and gray barber-pole striped tie in danger of falling from a display table. "Are the new ties selling well?"

Glancing at the tie she'd smoothed, he swallowed, sending his Adam's apple dancing. "Yes, ma'am. Especially the C-Coakley line."

"My personal favorite," she said, pleased that the line of ties her father had gruffly pronounced as "damnably expensive" were selling well despite the admittedly steep price tags. "Keep up the good work, Reggie."

Her chunky-heeled black leather pumps felt nice and solid against the polished marble floor as she walked toward the stairs. The stairs themselves, although a mainstay in her casual exercise program, were a bit of a test today in her shorter than usual skirt—black crepe with no slit. She climbed the four flights of stairs slowly to prevent perspiration from gathering on the paper thin indigo blouse beneath the black jacket. Near the top, she checked her watch. Nine-thirty. Just enough time to grab another cup of coffee and sift through the previous week's sales figures. Might as well head for the conference room early and claim a good vantage point. Things could get interesting, and she wanted a view.

Her secretary Tess, an efficient and animated young woman who studied fashion merchandising at night, was holding out the sales reports before Alex even reached the woman's desk.

"Thanks, Tess."

"You look tired."

So much for her new under-eye concealer. "I guess I need more caffeine."

"Let me get your coffee, Ms. Tremont." Despite Alex's numerous requests for Tess to call her by her first name, her secretary insisted on addressing her formally. Before Alex could protest, Tess had relieved her of the stoneware mug and refilled it with black Irish roast from a coffeemaker on a credenza. "Do you have anything for me to add to your agenda today?"

"No," Alex said, inclining her head in thanks as she took the mug. "Just be on the lookout for a Mr. Jack Stillman for the ten o'clock meeting, and show him to the boardroom, please."

"How will I know him?" Tess asked, her green eyes wide and interested.

Alex bit back a smirk. Her pretty secretary was a bit of a flirt, and always perked up when a man came around. Shaggy Jack Stillman was probably right up her alley, too.

"Believe me, you can't miss him." She shook her head good-naturedly as she walked down the hall to the executive conference room, nodding good morning to a half-dozen peers and subordinates as she went. Tess ran through men like most women ran through panty hose.

Alex frowned down at her own durable black hose. Funny, she hadn't bought a new pair in ages.

At the door to the conference room, she hesitated only a second before stepping inside. In her opinion, these four walls encompassed the most unappealing space in the entire five-story building. Alex had attempted to overhaul the depressing room many times, but she'd finally tired of butting heads with her father, who insisted the conference room be left as is. *As is,* however, was an oppressive collection of dark, clubby wood bookshelves studded with sports paraphernalia. A thoroughly masculine domain, the three darkly paneled walls adorned with gaping fish frozen into curling leaps, and worse, two antlered deer heads. Alex felt nauseous every time she looked at the poor creatures.

The furniture wasn't much better, the bulky chairs so unwieldy she could barely move them in and out from the broad-legged table. She chose the chair at the head of the table, farthest from the door. After setting down her coffee cup and the reports, she crossed the gloomy room to open the window blinds on the outside wall. As far as she was concerned, the sole good feature of the room was the view.

Rolling hills of pasture land and forests provided a backdrop for the modest Lexington skyline. The fiery October hues threw the white board fences encircling distant grazing land into stark relief. The flying hooves of two yearlings sprinting across a slanted field reminded her that fall horse racing season at Keeneland started in a couple of days. Alex smiled, momentarily distracted, and experienced a rush of gratitude to be living in such a beautiful area.

Winding, tree-lined roads led residents into the downtown area, a myriad of old tobacco warehouses, new office buildings, slender town houses and fountained courtyards. Brick, stone, metal, concrete, glass, water, one- and two-way streets—all these elements combined to create the casual, eclectic cityscape that embodied Lexington: part urban, part rural, totally accommodating.

Tremont's flagship store and administrative offices occupied a five-story building on Webster Avenue just a few blocks from the center of downtown, and walking distance from Alex's loft apartment. They had managed to compete with the malls by building an adjacent parking structure and, at her persistent urging, by developing a food court on the entire first floor of the building, including a sidewalk café that had become very popular with the business lunch crowd and the Junior League. As a result, gift shops and service businesses had popped up all around them.

Alex sipped her coffee, feeling very much like a proud parent admiring her offspring. She had contributed to the growth of Tremont's, and Tremont's played a vital role in the downtown economy. Long after she was gone, Tremont's would be a living, breathing entity, a legacy of her father's and her own and her children's impact on the city and the state. The knowledge pleased her immensely.

As she stared down at the street, a red taxicab pulled alongside the opposite sidewalk, and a man alighted. Bound for the financial building two doors down, she suspected, then she squinted to study the man in the distance as he leaned inside to pay the driver. He certainly looked the part of a money man—commanding figure, dark hair, proper suit. Her tongue poked deep into her cheek. And he wasn't a bad-looking fellow, either.

"What's so interesting?"

She dropped the blind, turned, and conjured up a smile for Heath Reddinger, who looked fair and fit and smart in his navy pinstripe suit and tortoiseshell-rimmed glasses. "Just people-watching."

His forehead furrowed. "Alex, you look tired. I thought you were going to bed early last night."

"I did," she said, telling herself she should feel flattered by his concern rather than faintly annoyed. "I'm fine, really."

Heath glanced back toward the door to ensure they were alone. They both agreed not to flaunt their relationship during work hours. "I'm sorry, but I have to cancel dinner tonight," he said. "I just discovered I'm needed in Cincinnati. I'm leaving this afternoon."

"For how long?" She'd been looking forward to a relaxing evening together, and to the sea bass at Gerrard's.

"No more than a couple of days, I think."

Alex frowned. "A problem with our bank?"

Heath sipped his creamed coffee before he answered. "No problem, just an issue. Can I get a rain check on dinner?"

She nodded, respectful of Heath's dedication to her father's company.

Heath reached forward and smoothed a finger back from her temple. "Maybe we should plan a long weekend away when I get back, hmm?"

A light rapping on the door accompanied by Tess clearing her throat diverted Alex's attention over Heath's shoulder. The flash of irritation that her secretary had been privy to the intimate gesture and conversation was quickly replaced by her puzzlement at the tall gentleman standing next to a beaming Tess. A memory cord stirred at the base of Alex's brain, and she realized the dark-headed visitor was the same man she'd watched climb out of the taxi on the street below. A salesman, of course. What else would a man as handsome as he be doing for a living? Riveting dark eyes, tanned, planed features, immaculate suit. No wonder Tess looked like she'd been plugged into an electrical transformer. Alex grudgingly indulged in a twinge of appreciation of her own—the man was...noteworthy.

Alex stepped around Heath. "Yes, Tess?"

"Mr. Stillman is here."

Alex blinked, wondering why Tess had announced Stillman's arrival before introducing the salesman. Her gaze darted to the man, and one side of his mouth curved upward. Confusion flooded her.

"Good morning, Ms. Tremont," the man said in a hauntingly familiar voice.

5

A FULL FIFTEEN SECONDS passed before Alex made the connection that this...paragon...was the same wild-eyed, bushy-headed, scruffy-faced irreverent vagrant she'd spoken to yesterday. Her jaw loosened a bit, and her mind raced, trying to reconcile the two images.

Meanwhile, Jack Stillman seemed to be enjoying every minute of her discomfort. His dark eyes—brown? green?—alight with the barest hint of amusement, never left her face. Her heart pumped wildly, sending hot apprehension to her limbs while alarms sounded in her ears. His full-fledged grin catapulted his unnerving energy across the space between them to wrap around her. Alex resisted the pull, leaning into the conference room table until the hard edge bit into the front of her thighs. This man was dangerous, and she would do well to keep her distance, and to keep her wits about her.

"Good morning, Mr. Stillman," she replied coolly, then gestured toward the opposite end of the table. "Won't you have a seat?" Getting the man off his feet would give her the slightest advantage.

Instead of answering, he strode toward Heath and extended his hand. "Jack Stillman of the Stillman & Sons Agency."

Heath introduced himself, and Alex could have kicked herself for her gaffe. The men shook hands, although the set of Heath's chin emanated a certain wariness. Bobby Warner, a fellow sales director and her prime competition for the vice presidency walked in with his signature swagger, then gaped at Jack.

"You're not the Jack Stillman who played for UK in the early eighties?"

Jack dimpled. "Guilty."

Behind them, Alex rolled her eyes.

"I'll never forget that sixty-six-yard touchdown against Tennessee in eighty-four," Bobby said, stepping back to feign a catch while Alex stared. She could count on her colleagues to overlook Jack Stillman's exaggerated celebrity and do what was best for the company...couldn't she?

To her relief, several other associates entered the room—the public relations director, another sales director, two vice presidents and a couple of marketing assistants—chatting among themselves. She left the introductions to Bobby, who seemed disturbingly chummy with Jack Stillman after only three and a half minutes. The group body language concerned her. The men leaned toward him, hands in pockets, athletically wide-legged—even Rudy Claven, who hadn't missed being a woman by much, and was teased mercifully by the company softball team for "throwing like a girl." And the four women in the room seemed to hang on to every detail as Bobby ingratiatingly expanded on Jack's scoffing I'm-not-a-legend preamble.

Ugh.

Alex pretended to mingle as they waited for her father, but instead studied Jack from beneath her lashes, part of her marveling over his physical transformation, all of her wary to the point of nervous tension. He panned his audience to include everyone in a glory-days anecdote he'd probably recounted a thousand times, and his gaze seemed to linger on her longer than necessary.

Men were like cats, she observed, pretending to study her watch. The more you ignored them, the more they wanted your attention. She forced herself not to listen to Jack Stillman's words, although his baritone was impossible to shut out. Someone had found a photo of the '85 UK football team among the cluttered bookshelves, and there he was, Jack pointed out as everyone crowded around, then launched into a story about the fellow who sat next to him. Within seconds, everyone was laughing.

Oh, brother. Alex took a deep gulp of coffee and scalded her tongue. "Dammit!"

Her expletive coincided with a lull in the laughter and seemed to reverberate from the dark walls. Everyone turned to stare, including Jack, whose eyes danced with amusement as she ran her tender tongue against the roof of her mouth. She had the strongest urge to stick it out at him.

"Problem, my dear?" her father asked, strolling into the room with all the casual ease of a man who owned the floors, walls and ceilings. At last everyone fell away from Jack Stillman and headed toward the table, scrupulously avoiding the chair opposite Alex, reserved for her father, of course.

"No," she said somewhat thickly, walking around the table. "Allow me to introduce Mr. St—"

"*Jack Stillman,*" her father cut in, pumping the visitor's hand, his broad face creasing in a grin reserved only for the most privileged. "*Jack the Attack.*"

Alex wanted to heave.

"It's a pleasure to meet you, Mr. Tremont," Jack said, looking duly humbled.

"Aren't you in top form," her father said. "Nice suit, son. One of ours, I do believe."

Jack nodded and smoothed the sleeve of his charcoal-gray suit. "Your private label."

She'd been so distracted by the change in his appearance, she hadn't noticed he was wearing one of the most expensive suits they carried. Brownnoser.

"Nice tie, too," her father continued with an appraising nod.

Over his crisply starched white shirt, Jack was sporting a tie identical to the gray and navy barber-pole striped one she'd fingered earlier this morning, one in the line her father had scoffed at, but suddenly thought was "nice."

Her father turned to the assembled group and beamed while clapping Jack on the back. "He wears our clothes. The man is talented *and* smart."

They obliged with a round of laughter while Alex fumed. As far as she was concerned, the man was a fraud, and his presentation would undoubtedly reflect his ineptitude. After all, clothes did *not* make the man.

"Shall we start the meeting?" she asked over the din, irritated when Jack sat next to her father. Darn it, she should have separated them, she realized too late. Luckily Tess arrived with the presentation easel, so Alex directed her to set it up on her end of the room. Her secretary loitered, casting sideways glances at Jack Stillman until Alex cleared her throat meaningfully.

Once the door closed, Alex took a deep breath. "Okay, everyone, let's get this over wi—" She stopped abruptly, feeling a flush creep up her neck as surprised looks darted her way. Alex hesitated, half afraid her father would jump to his feet and assume control of the meeting. But his face was remarkably placid.

"I mean, let's begin," she amended smoothly. "As you know, Tremont Enterprises is looking for a new advertising agency to take the company into the millennium." Pausing for effect, she tried to inject just the right amount of doubt into her tone. "Mr. Jack Stillman of the Stillman & Sons Agency is here today to convince us that his small, family-owned business can handle an account the size of Tremont's."

At the tightening of his jaw, she saw her veiled barb had

hit home. "Mr. Stillman, perhaps you can tell us more about yourself and your company." As she took her seat, Alex gave him a tight smile that said she would reveal him at the earliest convenience for the con man he was. "After all," she added, "not everyone was treated to the, um, *enlightening* reception I received yesterday."

His smile was sublime as he stood and launched into a brief background of his family business, including his and his brother's degrees from UK, and the recent addition of a large regional natural food manufacturer to their client list. Distinctly unimpressed, Alex was hiding a yawn behind her hand when he looked her way. "But I'm glad you brought up your visit to my office, Ms. Tremont, because it dovetails perfectly into my presentation for today."

She realized he was waiting for a response, so she obliged with as little interest as possible. "Oh?"

Jack's mouth twitched as his gaze bore into her. "You see...my plan worked perfectly."

As his words sunk in, Alex sobered with a sense of impending doom. "What plan would that be?"

He stroked his chin thoughtfully as he walked around her father's chair. She caught a glint of silver in his hair when he stepped through a shaft of sunlight. "What was your impression of me yesterday, Ms. Tremont?"

The dark walls of the room suddenly seemed closer, and the hairs at the nape of her exposed neck tingled. "The truth?"

His eyes glittered. "Absolutely."

Alex pursed her lips. How could she best put into words that she found him to be a very base individual who might be more at home digging a ditch and ogling female pedestrians than playing at running a business? Studying his smooth, too-confident face, she decided that Jack Stillman needed to be taken down a notch. Or three. "Frankly, I found you to be rather odious."

Eyebrows shot high around the table, accompanied by sharp gasps and a titter or two. "Alex!" her father admonished, but she didn't break eye contact with Jack. This was personal.

Her opponent's smile was patient. "Why?"

In her peripheral vision, she saw heads pivot back and forth between them, but as far as Alex was concerned, she and Jack were the only two people in the room. An invisible tunnel connected them across the table. She felt an alarming draw to her energy, as if the space wasn't big enough for the both of them. With effort, she matched his smile. "You mean other than the fact that you were rude and boorish?"

Bodies shifted.

He spread his large hands. "My apologies if you were offended, but I believe you were reacting to something other than my words."

"Such as?" she asked dryly.

"My appearance?"

Alex blinked, but didn't reply.

"In fact," Jack said, walking around the table toward her. "You didn't recognize me when I arrived today, did you, Ms. Tremont?"

Irritated, she crossed her arms. "You do look quite different, Mr. Stillman."

He turned to address everyone else. "Just so you'll know, when Ms. Tremont came by yesterday, I was wearing cutoff shorts, a Hawaiian shirt and a tool belt."

What was he up to? "You forgot the bad tie and the fact that you were barefoot," she supplied, shoving her shoulders back into the stiff chair. Chuckles circled the table, but she remained stoic.

"Ah, you *are* observant." He graced her with a charming smile, then gestured to himself, sweeping his hand down his torso as he walked closer still. "Would you say my appearance today is an improvement?"

Hot anger shot through her, and her eyes traveled the length of him as if they had a mind of their own. Standing almost within touching distance, Jack Stillman was one gorgeously put together man, but she wasn't about to give him undue credit for lucking into a favorable gene pool. "Anything would be an improvement."

His answer was a devilish grin of concession, which drew more light laughter from the table.

Alex didn't appreciate being put in the hot seat—especially when she'd planned to be roasting Jack Stillman right about now. "Mr. Stillman, I assume you have a point?"

"Ah," he said, raising a finger and lifting the portfolio he'd leaned against the wall, then placing it on the easel. "My point is that a certain old saying has credence." With a flick of his wrist, he unsnapped the little strap that held together the worn leather portfolio, and Alex stifled a scoff. A large hand-painted color poster showed a man in a football uniform throwing a pass, cheering fans behind him.

Jack lowered the panel to reveal another poster showing the same man wearing chinos and a casual shirt flipping burgers on a grill, a couple of admiring women standing nearby with umbrella'd drinks. The next poster showed the man in a suit carrying a briefcase and checking his watch as he hurried somewhere, again with a couple of female onlookers. The fourth poster showed the now shirtless man reclining in bed, wearing boxer shorts, a woman's hand resting on his shoulder. Her midsection stirred at the intimacy of the moment translated by the simplicity of the picture. She guessed he'd shown great restraint in not depicting *two* women's hands.

Her eyes strayed to Jack, unnerved that he seemed to be gauging her reaction. She kept her expression passive, and glanced away, not about to reveal that the picture conjured up images of Jack Stillman himself reclining in bed with a lover. She banished the disturbing thought and forbade herself from making such appalling slips in the future.

"My point, one that Ms. Tremont can attest to, is—" he encompassed the room with a tantalizing smile and flipped down the poster to reveal a slogan in neat black block letters "—Tremont's. Because clothes *do* make the man."

Alex thought her head might explode on the spot.

JACK HOPED NO ONE could hear his heart thrashing in his chest—the scheme of putting a creative spin on yesterday's fiasco was risky, but he had nothing to lose. It was fourth down with long yardage, and he'd been scrambling to find a seam in the end zone. The deadly look Alexandria Tremont gave him, however, was akin to taking the pigskin right between the eyes. Now his only hope was to escape the game without further injury. He eyed the distance between her and him, versus him and the door—could he make it?

The room crackled with expectant silence, then Al Tremont suddenly burst out laughing, clapping his fleshy hands. "I *like* it."

Jack exhaled the breath he'd been holding as the others, as if awaiting their boss's cue, began to hum and nod their approval. Heath Reddinger seemed noncommittal, but from what he had observed when he'd followed the secretary into the room, Reddinger and the fetching Alexandria were involved romantically. The thought stirred a different kind of competitive urge in Jack's stomach. Now Reddinger darted looks toward his ladylove, waiting for a glance of...permission? Poor sap.

Apparently Alexandria wasn't influenced by her father's favorable opinion. "Excuse me," she said in a crisp tone as she swept her gaze over her colleagues. "Excuse me!"

Jack suspected if she'd had a gavel within reach, she would have banged the table top, but everyone fell silent and gave her their attention.

She pressed her lips together, as if gathering her composure, then spoke, her voice rich and controlled. "Frankly, I think the ad is a bit sexist. After all, our typical shopper is *female*, and we can't afford to alienate her."

"We wouldn't be alienating her," Jack said, speaking as if he were already part of the Tremont's team. He withdrew a television commercial storyboard of a woman shopping in the men's department. "Instead we'd be saying, 'Come into Tremont's and outfit your man in style.'"

Outfit your man? She narrowed her eyes at him. "I repeat for the benefit of the hard-of-hearing, I think the idea is sexist, and if I were the customer, I would be offended."

Jack felt perversely compelled to provoke her, although he wasn't sure why. "But you, Ms. Tremont, are not the typical female customer." Reciting from memory the demographics hastily gathered from Reggie over the taxi driver's cell phone, he said, "Correct me if I'm wrong, but I believe the typical customer is both younger *and* married."

He had hit a nerve—maybe two.

While Alexandria turned a becoming shade of crimson, Al Tremont laughed again, slapping his knee. "He's got you there, Alex."

Alex. The name suited her, Jack decided, then he plunged ahead. "She is also less educated and less successful," he added, hoping to placate her, although from the set of her mouth, he hadn't. "But she spends a disproportionate amount of her disposable income on clothing. I think we can entice her to spend even more of her own money—" he grinned "—or someone else's—"

More laughter sounded, accompanied by nods.

"—buying clothes for her man."

"Clothes for her man?" Alex's tone was heavy with disdain. "Mr. Stillman, that thinking smacks of chauvinism."

"Maybe," he conceded. "But how are menswear sales?"

"We don't divulge sales figures to outsiders."

"Menswear sales are lousy," Al Tremont offered.

"But improving," Alex insisted, gripping the edge of the table and shooting her father a withering glance.

"I assume profit margins are higher for men's clothing to compensate for the lower volume," Jack continued, trying to smooth the brewing disagreement between father and daughter. "So it makes sense to target an underselling, high-margin department. Present a campaign specifically designed to bring women into the store to shop for the men in their lives, and they're sure to wander into other departments."

"We could put cross-promotional materials for women's wear, children's and housewares in the men's department," one of the young women offered.

Jack remembered she was an assistant in marketing. "Great idea," he said, and was rewarded with a blushing, shy grin. "Coax them into other departments after they've finished shopping in menswear."

Side conversations erupted around the table. Jack could see the idea catching and spreading. Alex sat rigidly in her chair, eyeing her associates.

"Mr. Stillman, do you have any experience in producing television commercials?" Heath Reddinger asked, restoring the room to relative quiet.

Good old Heath—offering a bit of disguised resistance for Alex's sake. "No," he admitted. "But I do have a relationship with a local producer, who does top-notch work." A chance glance at Alexandria revealed her too-blue eyes had rolled upward, so he directed the rest of his remarks to her father.

"I recommend that you contract a male model exclusively for Tremont's, then flood the media with his image."

Tremont was nodding. "I like it—simple, straightforward, smart."

Alexandria cleared her throat noisily. "It's not the level of sophistication I had in mind for the store. I wanted to spotlight our women's designer clothing, our fine jewelry, cosmetics—"

"Alex," her father cut in, his face stern. "I think we should take Jack's proposal under serious consideration."

"Perhaps," she returned across the table, her own expression firm, "we should ask *Jack* to leave the room so we can discuss the pros and cons among ourselves."

Jack moved toward the door, but Al Tremont held up his hand. "Stay, son. I just need to know how much all this is going to cost."

"Father," Alex said, rising, her eyes wide. "This matter is far too important to be decided unilaterally in mere minutes. Remember, we have other agencies to interview, and besides, the entire marketing team should convene and discuss—"

"Alex," her father said abruptly, his mouth set in a frown, his double chin shaking, "I've made up my mind, and it's the Stillman agency I want!"

Although the words were music to his ears, Jack was aware of awkwardness vibrating between the walls, and for a moment, he felt a pang of sympathy for Alexandria. The man did seem to be a bit overbearing, and Jack was curious to see how she would respond.

"Father, a word with you outside?" To her credit, her tone was sweet, but he detected a slight tremor. She marched toward the door and exited, head high, leaving the door ajar. Jack and everyone else shifted their glance toward Al Tremont, who sighed heavily, then pushed himself to his feet and followed her, muttering under his breath.

ALEX PACED IN THE HALLWAY, shaking with a level of anger she hadn't experienced since discovering her father was going to marry Gloria the Gold Digger scarcely a year after her precious mother's death. How dare he undermine the authority he'd given her mere weeks ago! And in front of colleagues and other vice presidents, no less—not to mention that abominable Jack Stillman. *Clothes do make the man.* How lame. Thoughts of what she would do if her father didn't follow her were cut short by his appearance.

"Alex, what is the meaning of this?"

She crossed her arms. "I was going to ask you the same thing. The last time I looked, choosing an advertising agency fell under my area of responsibility." Gesturing toward the conference room, she said, "I can't believe you would just hand over our account to that inept man!"

"Imagine," her father murmured, a nostalgic smile on his broad face. "Jack the Attack working for me."

Incredulous, Alex's mouth worked up and down in alarm. He was dismissing her opinion on this critical matter? "Dad, surely you're not willing to jeopardize our advertising campaign, possibly our entire holiday sales season, simply to hire that has-been jock?"

He clasped her hand between his two. "Alex, dear, the man is talented, and he has a catchy idea that the rest of the staff likes."

"They're just humoring you."

"Then I wish you would, too," he said, adopting a heart-melting smile.

"Dad—"

"Alex, do this one thing for me. Work with Jack Stillman to get this campaign off the ground and let's see where it goes."

"But the timing...it's so risky—"

"And sometimes it takes a rebel to shake things up," he said, then looked contrite. "Sweetheart, I'm sorry I raised my voice in there, but I think you had your mind made up before the man even walked in."

"Dad, if you could have seen him yesterday—"

"And now we know why he looked the way he did, to make a point."

Alex scoffed. "That's impossible—he had no idea I was dropping by. On top of everything else, the man's a pathological liar."

"I like the boy, and my gut tells me this is the right thing to do, but it won't work unless you get on board."

"Oh, you need me now?" She hated the hurt she couldn't seem to keep out of her voice.

His smile was indulgent. "Of course, sweetheart. I won't offer Stillman the contract unless you agree to monitor the campaign."

A warm, fuzzy feeling lodged beneath her heart, and she smiled in spite of their disagreement. How she loved this man—her mentor, her hero. She couldn't dispute the fact that his business judgment was *usually* sound, although she had an ominous feeling about this particular decision.

"In fact—" he winked "—taking on this kind of project will prove what a team player you are, my dear."

The vice presidency—was he dangling his endorsement in front of her? Alex sank her teeth into her lower lip.

"What do you say?" he asked, squeezing her hand. "Help me keep my promise to Jack's father. I have a feeling their business could use a life preserver."

"More like a crash cart," she observed dryly.

"So you'll do it? For me?"

The last vestiges of her anger dissolved and she nodded, amenable to a compromise. "But only for two weeks. If the focus group doesn't like what Jack Stillman comes up with, then we cut ties with him and interview the St. Louis firm."

Her father beamed. "That's my girl." With his hand on her waist, he steered her back in the direction of the boardroom. Alex felt buoyed, willing to accept full credit for his good cheer.

Resigned to the unpalatable task before her, Alex inhaled

deeply and followed him back into the room, aware of the anxious glances from the table. Al walked up to stand beside Jack, pulling Alex close to him on the other side. Behind her father's shoulders, she caught Jack Stillman's mocking gaze and wondered how she'd keep from socking him over the next fourteen days.

"I'm happy to report," her father said, his eyes shining, "that Alex and I have reached a compromise to give Mr. Stillman the opportunity to impress us, and I'm sure that, just like on the football field, Jack won't let us down."

Jack inclined his head to acknowledge the smattering of polite applause. "I'll do my best, sir."

Two weeks, Alex told herself, forcing a smile to her lips. She could walk on hot coals for two weeks if she had to. And it wasn't like they'd have to be together every minute—after all, Jack wouldn't be involved in *every* aspect of the project. He would simply hand off his ideas to the photographer and the producer of the commercials, for instance. She could take it from there. Yes...things weren't so bad.

"In fact," her father continued, his face animated. "I just had an inspiration! Who needs to look for a male model when we have Jack the Attack?"

Alex's stomach vaulted. "What?"

"What?" Jack asked at the same time.

"Why, it's perfect," Al continued, gesturing to Jack with both hands as if he were presenting a refrigerator to a studio audience. "*Jack* will be the spokesman for Tremont's. He'll be the star of our commercials!"

He clapped Jack hard on the back, but Alex was the one who felt as if her heartbeat needed a jump start. *Jack Stillman*, the Tremont's spokesman? She opened her mouth to scream no, but her voice had fled—apparently to join her father's good sense.

And her father had eyes only for Jack. Puffed up with pride, he beamed at his new recruit. "How about it, son?"

Al turned and gestured to some invisible horizon, his thumb and forefinger indicating a name in lights. "Just imagine, when people see 'Tremont's,' they'll think of 'Jack the Attack.'"

Alex's vision blurred. She mumbled something about an important conference call and walked out of the room as calmly as her knocking knees would allow. Her father was so preoccupied with his find, he'd never miss her. On the way to her office, mind reeling, she somehow managed to snag her panty hose on a rattan wastebasket.

Great. On top of everything else, now she had to buy new panty hose.

6

TUESDAY LAUGHED, her eyes wide. "You went over there flying by the seat of borrowed pants, and came back with the account *and* the starring role?"

Jack shrugged and loosened his tie. "The old man was so excited, I had no choice but to say yes."

"What's your brother going to say about you modeling?"

He frowned. "It's *not* modeling."

She quirked an eyebrow. "You going to put on their clothes and let people point a camera at you?"

He jammed his hands on his hips, ready to argue, then sighed and nodded.

"Sounds like modeling to me. You must have impressed them with the new you. How did Ms. Tremont react?"

"Not well," he admitted. In fact, the one dim spot of the day had been when he'd looked up from shaking Al Tremont's hand to find that Alex had disappeared. She had a prior appointment, her father had explained unconvincingly, then assured Jack he'd be seeing a lot of Alex in the next few days since she would serve as his liaison to the company. The news had stirred his stomach oddly. He'd wanted to speak to her, to extend an olive branch before he left, but Al had dismissed his daughter's reaction.

"She had her heart set on a fancy shmancy advertising outfit in St. Louis," he'd said. "Give her a few hours for the news to sink in, then call her to set up a time when the two of you can get together. I won't lie to you, son—she's a handful, but she's as smart as a whip. You're going to have to suck up a little to win her over, but I'm sure you can handle it." With that, Al, Heath Reddinger and Bobby Warner had whisked him off to an early and extended lunch.

At first, retelling football stories had been amusing, but after ninety minutes of constant prodding by Tremont and Warner, the enjoyment had worn mighty thin for Jack, and, he suspected, for Reddinger. Between the jokes, he had tried to glean as much business information as possible from the trio, but the sole kernel of interesting data was an overheard comment that Alexandria was left holding a dinner reservation for two at Gerrard's while Reddinger left town to handle a banking issue.

Jack had studied the men throughout the meal and concluded that Al Tremont was a risk-taker with enough wisdom to attract talented people—Jack liked him—that Bobby Warner was a quick study with enough wisdom to attract debate—Jack respected him—and that Heath Reddinger was a yes-man with enough wisdom to attract the boss's daughter—Jack *dis*liked him.

It was the sort of dislike one man felt for another man who had something the first man strongly thought the second man didn't deserve. Not that the first man *wanted* the something he thought the second man didn't deserve, it was just that the first man possessed an innate sense of justice.

"She didn't take it well at all," he repeated, half to himself.

Tuesday waved her hand. "She'll get used to having you around. Might be good for the both of you."

Jack frowned. "What's that supposed to mean?"

"Grown folk have to learn to get along with people they don't like."

"I never said I didn't like her."

"I was talking about *her* not liking *you*."

He bristled. "Why wouldn't she like me?"

Tuesday harrumphed. "You think because you put on

that fancy suit and got a haircut that the woman can't see through you?"

"You were the one who put me in this getup—under duress, I might add."

She wagged her finger in his direction. "You might have impressed the men, and maybe even the fickle women, but my guess is that after the way you treated Ms. Tremont when she came here, she'll be on her guard. Smart lady, judging by the way you conduct business."

"I got the account, didn't I?"

Tuesday snorted. "Sounds like they want your face more than your advertising talent."

"Gee, thanks for the vote of confidence."

"That's part of my job," she said with a shrug.

"Speaking of *your* job, there isn't one. We can't afford you."

"You can't afford *not* to have me," she replied, lifting both hands.

Frowning, Jack glanced around the front office, not a bit surprised to see that Tuesday had rearranged its contents in a more pleasing manner. A fresh but pungent odor permeated the air. "What's that smell?"

"Paint," she said, nodding toward the yellow walls. "I thought this room could use a pick-me-up."

Jack stared at the clean, bright walls. What color had they been before? "*You* painted?"

Tuesday shrugged. "An apron, a gallon of paint, and a roller—no big deal. Besides, I was bored."

"Where did you get the supplies?" he asked suspiciously.

"Call it a contribution," she said. "I wanted to make this room more comfortable."

"Well, don't get too comfortable," he warned. "There *is* no job."

She sniffed, disregarding him completely.

Jack frowned. "When is Mr. Stripling supposed to arrive?"

She nodded toward the back office. "He's been here for an hour—I gave him another back adjustment and sat him at Derek's desk. He wants to talk to you a-s-a-p about missing quarterly tax payments." Tuesday extended a hand-written note which presumably held the man's instructions.

Jack glared and snatched the piece of paper. "Keep your hands off our auditor! Anything else?"

Tuesday walked around the desk she had made her own, complete with a nameplate—where had *that* come from?—and picked up a handful of pink phone message slips. "Donald Phillips wants you to review new pages to the company's website."

"I don't suppose he said anything about sending us a check," Jack grumbled.

"It arrived today."

"Great. We need to—"

"Pay the phone bill, the electric bill, Lamberly Printing, the post office box rental, Beecher's Office Supplies and three returned check charges from the bank." She smiled and handed him a stack of papers. "Counter-sign the check for deposit, then sign all the checks I filled out."

"I'm not giving you this check to deposit," he declared. "I hardly *know* you."

Without missing a beat, Tuesday picked up her purse and swung it over her shoulder. "I wasn't offering," she said, enunciating each word. "The rest of your phone messages are there for you to read yourself, and envelopes for the bills are already addressed and stamped."

Jack felt a little contrite as she walked toward the door, her hips swaying with attitude. "Where are you going?"

"Home," she tossed over her shoulder. "I'm taking the rest of the afternoon off."

"You don't have a job to take time off *from*," he reminded her grumpily.

"See you tomorrow, model man."

Jack massaged the bridge of his nose, then carried the handful of papers with him to the back office. Mr. Stripling sat at Derek's desk surrounded by files and folders, with a boardlike device strapped to his back, his face arranged in an unpleasant expression.

"Good day, Mr. Stripling."

The man scowled in his direction. "Is it? I hadn't noticed, having been assaulted once again by your office manager and left to sit here all afternoon wracked with unbearable pain."

Jack swallowed a smile at the image of Tuesday pinning the slight man down long enough to crack his neck—again. Hadn't the man seen it coming this time? "I apologize, Mr. Stripling, but that unstable woman does *not* work for us."

"So you've said, and I find the entire situation quite suspect."

Jack flung his arm toward the files the man was delving into. "You'll see—there's no record of having a Tuesday Humphrey on our payroll."

"Which means you've been paying her under the table," Stripling chirped. "A crime in and of itself."

"No—" Jack held up his hand, then stopped. "Forget it," he mumbled, crossing to his own desk where he tossed the stack of bills. "I've got more important things to worry about."

If possible, the man stiffened even more, and his bow tie practically twitched. "More important than the IRS?"

"Yeah," Jack said, falling into his seat. "An irate woman."

"Your office manager?"

"No," he said, picking up the phone to dial Derek. "A different irate woman. I seem to be collecting them."

As the phone rang on the other end, his spirits lifted in anticipation of telling his brother the news about the account, but he debated telling Derek that he had also been asked to be the Tremont's spokesman. He didn't want to give Derek the impression that he might sacrifice the work of the agency to satisfy this spokesman gig. Besides, Tuesday had pricked a concern he'd been harboring since leaving Tremont's—perhaps Al Tremont was more intrigued by the thought of Jack the Attack doing commercials for the department store than the thought of Jack Stillman doing advertising work for the department store.

"Hello, this is Derek."

"Hi, bro. Did I catch you at a bad time?"

"Jack, thank goodness! I've been going crazy waiting to hear from you. How'd the meeting go with Tremont?"

"We got the account."

"That's great!" Derek whooped and lowered the mouthpiece to yell the news to someone else—presumably his wife Janine—then returned. "How long is the contract for?"

"Two weeks."

"Two weeks?" Disappointment filtered his brother's voice. "Is that *all*?"

Rankled, Jack said, "It was the best I could do under the circumstances."

"What circumstances?"

"The decision to go with our agency wasn't unanimous."

"Did Mr. Tremont like the presentation?"

"Yeah, he liked it fine. It was his daughter who had a problem with it, and she's the director of sales and marketing."

"Daughter? What's she like?"

Jack's pulse spiked. "Young and hostile."

Derek emitted a thoughtful sound. "Pretty?"

His shrug was for himself, he supposed. "If you like the white-and-uptight type. I have two weeks to impress her, and if I do, we go back to the negotiating table."

"I'm coming home right away."

Panic gripped him—the last thing he wanted was for Derek to come home and find him making commercials. Two weeks would give him time to get a handle on the details. "Derek, man, don't do that," he said, laughing and forcing a casual tone. "Trust me, I'll have this thing well on its way by the time you get home. Enjoy the rest of your honeymoon."

"Are you sure?"

"Absolutely." He spent the next few minutes describing the concept of the ad campaign, then assured him—ignoring the unfriendly look that Stripling shot his way—that the audit was going smoothly and that the crazy lady who had made herself their office manager was gone. He didn't add "for the day."

"Jack," Derek said, his voice dipping. "I'm proud of you."

Touched and a little shaken, Jack scoffed. "Don't go getting all mushy on me. The business isn't in the bag yet."

"You just have to impress this Tremont lady, huh?"

"Yeah, but she's an uppity princess."

"Single?"

"I didn't ask," Jack hedged, knowing she was single—ergo Reddinger.

"Just be on your best behavior, okay?" Derek pleaded. "Don't try to be starting something."

"That's crazy," Jack protested. "I wouldn't—"

"Yes, you *would*. If you haven't noticed, little brother, you have a way of sabotaging your own success."

Jack sighed. "Relax, she has a boyfriend."

"Ha! Never stopped you before."

"Oh, and this coming from a guy who married the bride-to-be of a friend of his."

Derek grunted. "Steve and I aren't friends."

"Wonder why?"

"Okay, Jack, okay. But I'm telling you—stay away from this woman's bed."

"My contact with Alex Tremont will be limited to her wiping her six-hundred dollar stiletto shoes on my back."

"Promise me."

"Promise you what?"

"Promise me you won't become involved with this woman."

"What? No!"

"Then I'm coming home."

"No!" Jack sighed, then turned his back to the eavesdropping auditor and cupped his hand over the mouthpiece. "Okay."

"Okay, what?"

He rolled his eyes heavenward and lowered his voice even more. "Okay. I promise I won't become involved with...this woman."

"Great. I know I can trust you to keep your word to me, Jack."

Derek's words reverberated in his head long after he hung up the phone. By the time he signed all the outgoing checks and sealed the envelopes, Mr. Stripling was ready to leave. Jack helped him to his car while doing his best to ignore the man's ominous comments about missing forms and late payments. He assured the man they would discuss it later. Then Jack locked the office, rode his motorcycle to the bank to make the deposit, and dropped the bills into a mailbox.

Maneuvering through five o'clock traffic, he acknowledged he hadn't yet called Alex to set up a time to meet with her as her father had suggested. He also acknowledged that just the thought of seeing her again sent the blood rushing to the lower portions of his body. And irritation to nerve endings elsewhere.

He dreaded talking to the woman on the phone, knowing

she'd probably resist every opportunity to meet with him. Her father's words came back to him. *You're going to have to suck up a little to win her over, but I'm sure you can handle it.* Jack had never had to suck up to a woman in his life, and Alex Tremont didn't strike him as someone susceptible to sucking up anyway. Dammit, he'd have to be clever, which meant this was going to be a lot of work.

He sighed heavily, then from nowhere an idea popped into his mind. With growing confidence, Jack smiled and revved toward home, telling himself that just because he was already anticipating seeing Alex again did *not* mean he was going back on his promise to Derek.

7

ALEX KICKED OFF HER SHOES and removed the pins from her hair, lightly massaging her scalp as she finger combed the waves. Taking stock of her physical well-being, she acknowledged wryly that her feet hurt, her back hurt and her hair hurt. On a scale of one to ten for bad days at the office, she gave this day a nine, saving ten for the distinction of being fired.

Noticing the flashing light on her voice recorder, she pushed the play button as she walked past.

"Alex, this is Lana. You have to help me, I'm begging you. Vile Vicki is hip to me borrowing her things to get her back for borrowing *my* things. I need to stash a few valuables at your place until I can off her and dump the body."

Shaking her head at her friend's nonsense, she attempted a laugh, but in light of her abysmal day at the office, the noise came out sounding a bit strangled. After the farce of a meeting to "investigate" Jack Stillman's company as a potential advertising firm, she'd received preliminary reports from a reputable retail research firm that Tremont's was definitely losing sales ground, even worse considering that one of their main competitors was holding steady, and the other was posting significant gains.

What a time to be flushing their advertising dollars down the drain.

Before it slipped her mind, Alex dialed Lana's number—she and Vile Vicki were way beyond sharing a phone number—and left her a message to use the spare key and deposit her valuables in the antique chest she used as a coffee table, adding that Lana simply could not, however, hide Vicki's body in the chest. She hung up, thinking the couch looked extremely inviting, but she needed to eat, and the sole food items in the refrigerator—a jar of pimento olives and the carton of leftover fudge icing—would not suffice.

She also refused to stay in simply because Heath had left town. Irked for no reason she could put her finger on, she paced the perimeter of her apartment, peering out the windows at early dusk, feeling jittery. She sat down at her mother's mahogany baby grand piano showcased in the window of her loft, aching with the need to talk to her mother, to solicit her wisdom.

Life was pulling at her—Heath wanted to set a date, the pressures at the store had grown exponentially, Al wanted her to bond with Gloria while she yearned only for her father's affection. And now this liaison with Jack Stillman that went against her every instinct. The man oozed trouble, and she had the distinct feeling that the situation would become much more complicated before leveling out.

Alex pinged on a key or two with a sad smile—considering the few rusty tunes she could play, turning on the groaning faucet in the bathroom seemed simpler.

Suddenly she brightened, deciding that this evening would be the perfect time to indulge in her long-unfulfilled desire to ride again—to climb onto the back of a horse like when she was a child and bring the animal to a gallop.

She hadn't ridden in over a decade, but lately the longing to lean into the wind and feel her hair whipping her neck had recurred with more frequency. Lana said the urge for unbridled freedom was a by-product of becoming engaged, an explanation which Alex had dismissed. All she knew at the moment was that a therapeutic ride this evening would erase the stubborn image of Jack Stillman's smug, handsome face and her father's grating words, *When people see "Tremont's," they'll think of "Jack the Attack."*

Not the person who bore the name of his store, the person who had devoted her entire life to his business, the person who spent sleepless nights mulling strategies to grow sales, to eke another half percent out of their margins. Not *her*, but Jack Stillman.

She stomped to a bookcase, yanked out the yellow pages, then flipped to the *H*'s, only to be interrupted by a telltale frenzied knock on the door. Loath to answer Lana's certain questions about Jack, she nonetheless recognized the futility of postponing the inevitable. Still holding the phone book, she undid the chain and swung open the door. But the sight of the figure standing in the hallway stunned her into silence.

Holding a black motorcycle helmet beneath his arm, Jack Stillman inclined his dark head, his green-brown eyes dancing. "Good evening."

Her first impulse was to slam the door in his face, but she resisted. "The evening just took a decided turn for the worse," she said wryly. "How did you find my apartment?"

He gestured to her hand. "A brilliant invention, which I see you also utilize—the phone book."

His gaze swept over her, lingering on her loosened hair, traveling down to her stockinged feet. She tingled, and curled under her toes, mortified to be caught so completely off guard by the man she was supposed to "monitor," according to her father. "A gentleman would have called first."

He winked. "Ah, finally we agree on something—I'm not a gentleman."

A threat? A promise? "What are you doing here?" she blurted. Besides looking impossibly handsome, that is. His white cotton shirt, unbuttoned just enough to reveal the top of a snowy undershirt, was tucked into plain-front khaki chinos, belted with a thick black leather belt that matched his low-heeled boots and slightly worn leather jacket. Seasoned, generic clothes that might have come from Goodwill for all she knew, but devastatingly appealing on his lean frame. The split-second observation gave her a jarring glimpse into how the man might come across in a commercial.

He grinned—oh, Lord, a cleft in his chin, too.

"Your father suggested that you and I get together to talk about the ad campaign, and after the meeting today, I thought maybe it would be better if we got together in a more casual setting."

She pursed her lips, warily considering him and his offer. "Such as?"

"Such as Gerrard's?"

Alex blinked.

His laugh was mildly apologetic. "At lunch I overheard your fiancé tell your father that he'd made reservations before he had to leave town unexpectedly."

Funny that neither of the men had mentioned that they'd lunched with him, or for that matter, had invited her along. "How did you know Heath was my fiancé?"

He shrugged, his shoulders eclipsing the light from the hall. "I made an assumption based on the scene your secretary and I walked in on this morning and the rock on your finger."

"Oh." She rubbed her thumb on the underside of the ring, causing it to tilt and flash in the incandescent lighting. Symbolic of everything she wanted—if she married Heath, she could create her own loving family. Even her staid father wouldn't be able to resist the lure of grandchildren.

"Have you two set a date?"

Alex looked up and suddenly wondered if this playboy had children and ex-wives scattered about. He seemed too much of a big kid himself to be a good father, but then again, what did she know about good fathers? "I...I'd rather not discuss my personal business."

"Okay." He scratched at his temple, shifting his weight to his other foot. "So what about dinner—does Gerrard's work for you?"

The man had a lot of nerve assuming she didn't have something better to do like, like, like...where had she been planning to go? Oh, yes—horseback riding. She patted the phone book, glad for an out. "Sorry, I was on the verge of making other plans."

Before she realized his intention, he'd taken the book from her and turned to the page she'd held with her thumb. Her cheeks flamed as he scanned the listings.

"Hmm. Either you're looking to buy a new saddle, or you were planning to go horseback riding."

Feeling all of nine years old, Alex clasped her hands behind her back. "I, uh, was planning to go riding."

He closed the book and angled his head at her. "Well now, if it's a ride you're looking for, I can certainly oblige."

His throaty voice was free of innuendo, but his eyes told her the conversation could veer in any direction she wished to take it. In the course of a heartbeat, all kinds of naughty images galloped through her mind. She swallowed, squashing the imagery. The man was, after all, a professional flirt.

"Oh?" she asked lightly. "Do you own a horse?"

"Horse*power*," he corrected, setting the phone book on a table just inside the door. He patted his helmet. "Nothing like it—wind in your face, sun on your back, hugging the curves."

She almost smiled at the little-boy delight in his voice. The man was nothing if not compelling. His grin lit up his entire face, pushing up his sharp cheekbones, lifting his thick black brows, crimping the corners of his amazing eyes. He had a mischievous look that reminded her of a boy in her first grade class who had always talked her into stunts that resulted in either injury or punishment.

"I'd better not," she murmured, although even the hair on her arms strained toward him. "Besides, the restaurant probably already filled the reservation." In truth, the thought of sharing a meal alone with Jack Stillman unnerved her mightily.

"I checked, and they haven't." As if he sensed her wavering, he leaned forward, stretching his free arm to the other side of the jamb, filling the doorway. She caught a whiff of leather and a cologne unidentifiable to her well-trained nose. "Look, Alex, we got off on the wrong foot, and I'd like the chance to make it up to you."

Her nickname had rolled off his tongue so easily, she almost missed it. The implied familiarity rankled her, reminding her that she had much more at stake in the days ahead than Jack Stillman. A sobering flush warmed her neck. "Mr. Stillman, you assume too much. There's no need to 'make anything up' to me. Our relationship is and will continue to be strictly professional."

He held up one hand and laughed. "Whoa—I think we can both agree that the *only* thing we have in common is being blindsided by your father."

Alex straightened. Why did his corroboration with her statement seem like a thinly veiled insult? "My father tends to be impulsive."

He nodded. "And you take after your mother?"

His offhand reference to her dear mother struck yet another nerve. "I make my own way."

As if he sensed he'd stepped out of bounds, he gave her a rueful smile. "Let's face it, I need your support to make this a successful ad campaign. You and I might disagree on the means to the end, but we both have a vested interest in the end itself—more visibility for Tremont's."

A sliver of victory threaded through her chest as her mental footing returned. "Are you admitting, Mr. Stillman, that you can't do this without me?"

He laughed, a soft snort, then crossed his arms over his broad chest. "What I'm saying," he said, the bass in his voice rumbling in her ears, "is that we need each other."

There it was, that implication of intimacy that sent a chill up her back—not to be mistaken for a *thrill*, of course.

"But that's where we differ," she said with a tight smile. "You see, if *you* fail, then *I* will be proven right—that Stillman's isn't the ad agency for Tremont's."

He nodded, then pulled at his chin. "Except I suspect you're the kind of businesswoman who prefers to, um, *win* fair and square."

"This isn't a contest, Mr. Stillman."

His mouth twitched. "Oh, but isn't it? Father versus daughter?"

Alex swallowed hard, mortified that the stranger could see straight into her heart. "That's ridiculous. I only want what's best for the business."

She defied the urge to squirm under his probing gaze. Suddenly he smiled again and smacked the helmet in his hand, as if a decision had been reached. "Good, then we want the same thing, which is precisely why we should get started as soon as possible. Dinner is my treat."

She inhaled deeply, contemplating the ramifications of having dinner with this man in a highly public place where she and Heath were known as a couple. Then she realized that Gerrard's would be the most innocent of places for them to dine—no one could accuse them of a clandestine meeting.

"All right," she relented, injecting as much authority into her voice as possible. "But we go Dutch."

His smile wavered, but he nodded. "Wear something warm, night riding can be chilly."

Having a dinner meeting was one thing, but hanging on

to this man on the back of his bike? Alex shook her head. "Oh, no—I'm not climbing on that rattletrap motorcycle."

He shrugged. "Okay, if you'd rather I ride with you—"

"I'll meet you there," she said, then banged the door closed and exhaled.

THE WOMAN WAS A LITTLE short on charm, Jack decided as he glanced at the clock over the restaurant bar for the fifth time in as many minutes. He'd considered waiting outside her apartment complex until she emerged, then realized that some states would consider that stalking and, frankly, he didn't want to give Alex the impression that he would sit around waiting for her. With that thought, he sprang up from the barstool and leaned against the bar—he'd *stand* around waiting for her instead.

"Want another?" the bartender asked, pointing to his draft beer.

"No, thanks," Jack said, swirling the remainder of the ale in his glass.

The guy squinted, then his face broke into a wide smile. "Hey, you're Jack Stillman, aren't you?"

"Yeah."

The man stuck out his beefy hand and pumped Jack's. "Wow, this is a pleasure. What have you been doing, man?"

Jack adopted an accommodating expression. "This and that, mostly traveling."

"You back in town for good?"

"Good question." Jack pushed his empty glass forward, loathe to engage in a drawn-out conversation. Where the devil *was* she?

"Are you coaching?"

"Nope."

"Too bad, man. So what *do* you do?"

"My brother and I run an ad agency in town."

"Oh." The man nodded awkwardly, duly unimpressed. "You waiting for a dame?"

"How'd you know?"

"You got that hang-dog look."

He shot him an irritated frown.

"If you're interested," the man said, nodding across the room, "there's a sweet little redhead in the corner who's been trying to get your attention for a half hour."

Intrigued, and nursing a fair amount of spite toward the tardy Alexandria, Jack turned to check out the woman in question, quickly assessing she had all the bare essentials: height, curves and—most importantly—proximity. He twitched an eyebrow in her direction and was rewarded with a toss of hair and a dazzling smile. The redhead picked up her drink and walked toward him, a deep inhale away from splitting the seams of her faded jeans.

"Howdy," she drawled as she stepped up next to him at the bar.

He nodded a greeting. Knowing he'd never remember her name, he simply didn't ask.

She turned her back to the bar and leaned on her elbows. "You played football for UK, didn't you?"

Jack smirked. "You don't look old enough to have followed my career."

"I'm not. My father has an autographed picture of you in our rec room—it's been there since I was a kid."

Feeling ancient, Jack picked at peanuts from a dish on the bar.

"Buy me a drink?" she asked, pursing her bright pink mouth into a pretty pout.

"Looks like you're still working on that one," he said, nodding toward the frozen pink drink she held that coincidentally matched her binding pink T-shirt.

"I'm always planning ahead," she oozed, and leaned

closer as she laughed. At a loss, he manufactured a laugh, too.

"Did I miss something funny?"

Jack jerked around to find Alex standing behind them, her dark eyebrows high. He straightened, feeling ridiculously guilty, and conjured up an innocent smile. "No, just making conversation." He tossed a few bills on the counter, nodded to the redhead, then turned back to Alex. "Ready?"

She nodded, but from the pinched look around her lovely mouth, she was feeling guilty about meeting him...which meant she was capable of bending the rules. He grinned at the prim set of her shoulders as she walked three steps ahead of him all the way to the reservations station.

"What name?" the hostess asked.

"Reddinger," Alex said.

"Stillman," he said at the same time, which garnered a sharp look from his companion. At the hostess's perplexed expression, he added, "There's been a change from Reddinger to Stillman."

Alex shot him a suspicious frown and he winked back.

"Right this way."

He fell into step behind Alex as the hostess led the way to their table. She'd bound her hair again into a tight little wad, but had changed to loose, black dress jeans that hugged her hips and a turquoise silk blouse that shimmered under the lights as she walked. More than one man stole a glance as she walked between tables. Jack picked up his pace, his hand hovering near her waist of its own volition.

The hostess stopped at a secluded table for two near the enormous stone fireplace that held a fire, more for appearances than for heat. He beat Alex to her chair by a heartbeat and pulled it out for her.

"Thank you," she said, sounding wary as she allowed him to scoot the seat beneath her.

After handing them a wine list, the hostess disappeared,

replaced seconds later by a waiter. "Good evening, Ms. Tremont," he said, a genuine smile on his young face as he unfolded her napkin and draped it over her lap. But when he turned to Jack, he faltered a bit, obviously expecting someone else. So she and Reddinger were regulars, huh?

"Rick, this is Mr. Stillman," Alex supplied. "He's a..." she glanced over at Jack, making eye contact for two whole seconds "...business associate...of Mr. Reddinger's...and mine."

The waiter eyed him suspiciously, but nodded cordially enough.

"We'll have a bottle of chardonnay," she continued, setting aside the wine list.

"I'll take another beer," Jack said.

Alex eyed him as if he were a barbarian. "Bring a carafe of chardonnay for me," she amended with a small smile.

Once the waiter left, silence enveloped them. Jack attempted to catch her gaze, but it was as if an invisible iron gate had sprung up around her—she sat folded into herself, serene and stunning, as sleek as a cat, a different creature than the woman who had answered the door barefoot, on the verge of going horseback riding. The dichotomy intrigued him. "You look beautiful," he said before he could stop the words.

He got her attention, but she didn't appear particularly pleased. "Mr. Stillman—"

"Jack."

"—let's get down to business, shall we?"

Although he wanted nothing less than to talk about business, he said, "Sure. Where do you propose we begin?" She toyed with her empty wineglass, her engagement ring twinkling under the lights. Reddinger was a very lucky man.

"First things first," she said, leveling her ice-blue gaze at him. "You were lying this morning when you said that my visit to your office fit into some convoluted plan of yours. You had no way of knowing I would be stopping by."

"You can't prove that allegation," he said mildly, leaning his elbows on the table, etiquette be damned. God, she was gorgeous.

She lifted one delicate eyebrow. "I don't trust you."

He lowered his voice. "Are you normally this paranoid?"

One side of her mouth drew back. "Call me prudent."

The woman had lost her sense of humor somewhere between her apartment and the restaurant parking lot. "How about if we call a truce?" he asked, steepling his hands. "Just through dinner. Then we can go back to pecking each other to death if we want to."

She inhaled deeply, then released the breath in a long sigh. "Okay. I suppose the first thing we need to do is figure out how much can be feasibly delivered in the next two weeks."

"I'll follow your lead." *Anywhere you want to take me.* He blinked—where had that thought come from?

She pursed her mouth, and he could see the wheels turning in her pretty head. "I say we meet with the television producer and a photographer as soon as possible to shoot a cluster of spots around the—" she cleared her throat "—slogan."

Jack ignored her slight. "Meanwhile, I can polish the text for the print ads, come up with radio scripts, and shop around for billboard space."

"Then my team and I will coordinate internal promotions to complement the media efforts," she said with resignation in her voice. "We'll do the best we can with what we have to work with."

Jack gave her a wry smile. "You really should put a lid on your excitement."

The corners of her mouth curled up a fraction. "You might have blinded my father with your pseudo-celebrity, Mr. Stillman, but I'm a bit more skeptical. By signing your agency, my staff's work is multiplied. Believe it or not, baby-sitting you for the next two weeks isn't at the top of my wish list."

She leaned forward, offering a glimpse of her cleavage in the silky, button-up blouse. *Speaking of wish lists.* His promise to Derek was forgotten as lust flooded his limbs. He knew he was on shaky ground, but he opened his mouth anyway. "If it's any consolation, you're hands-down the best damn looking baby-sitter I've ever had.

8

SHAKEN DOWN to her sensible loafers, at first she thought she had misheard him. But one look at the raw invitation in Jack's eyes, and she knew she hadn't. How did one respond to such an overt remark? Sure, the feminine part of her was flattered, but the practical part of her was convinced he was playing her. He needed her cooperation, didn't he? The man probably knew only one way to influence women—between the sheets.

She opened her mouth to put him in his place, but the waiter arrived with her wine and his beer, then asked for their dinner order. Alex murmured she would have her usual, and Jack ordered a rare porterhouse steak, barbarian that he was. She capped her agitation and concentrated on steering the conversation back to business, finally pinning him down on a delivery date for the print ads. Within a few minutes, she felt as if she were regaining control.

"Will your brother be contributing to our account?" she asked, taking a larger swallow of wine than was probably wise on her empty stomach.

"Not creatively," Jack said. "Derek is more of a numbers man. And he's out of town for another couple of weeks on his honeymoon." Her expression must have given her away because he smiled and said, "You look surprised."

"I guess I assumed he was like you," she admitted, although she really didn't know what that was.

"You mean footloose and fancy free?"

So he wasn't attached. Alex lifted her glass to her mouth

and nodded, more interested in his answer than she cared to reveal.

"He was, up until a couple of months ago. Derek flew to Atlanta to stand in for me as best man at my college buddy's wedding, and ended up falling in love with the bride."

She choked on her wine, coughing and sputtering like an idiot. Jack stood and jerked on her arm as if she were three years old, and as if it would help at all. At last, she waved him away, still tingling where his big warm fingers had touched her. "You mean," she asked hoarsely, "that he stole his friend's fiancée?"

"Well, it's not as sordid as it sounds," he said. "They were trapped together in a hotel room under some kind of strange quarantine, and fell in love. Janine decided to call off the wedding, then a few weeks later, she and Derek reunited and were married."

Alex acknowledged the wine was going to her head because she actually cooed. "That's so romantic."

Jack shrugged, apparently less convinced. "I suppose."

"Is he like you in other ways?" She remembered the two of them in the yearbook, and wondered if they were as close as the picture portrayed.

He laughed and she registered alarming pleasure at the rumbling noise. "The similarity ends at the last name. Derek is serious, uptight, takes the weight of the world on his shoulders. But he's a great guy, and he seems really happy with Janine. She's good for him, I think. He's lightened up quite a bit."

She propped up her chin with her hand and watched him refill her wine glass from the carafe. "Where did they go?"

"Hawaii."

"That's nice," she murmured. She'd always wanted to go to Hawaii, but the timing had never seemed right to be away from the office. And now with the vice presidency on the line...

"A client we recently contracted with, Donald Phillips, has a condo on Maui. He was so pleased with the work Derek did on his account that he gave him the keys for an entire month."

"Honey."

Jack's head jerked up and his eyes widened. "What?"

"Honey," she repeated, reaching for her glass. "Donald Phillips's company makes honey. I went to school with his daughter."

He relaxed, then lifted his beer.

By the time the waiter delivered their food, Alex was feeling so relaxed herself, she was reluctant to indulge in her crab cake salad, and merely picked at it. Jack, on the other hand, dove into his steak and baked potato with such gusto, she had the feeling if he'd been by himself, he would have tucked his napkin into his shirt collar and dispensed with utensils. With no regard to the direction of her thoughts, she silently compared the man sitting across from her to Heath.

Jack Stillman was a man's man, big and angular and earthy, with a presence that would put most people at ease—most people who *liked* him, she clarified quickly. Heath, conversely, was precise and scholarly, with a presence that put most people on their best behavior. Jack had a wildness about him, from the way he talked to the way he carried himself across a room. She wondered if he realized that nearly every woman in the restaurant was captivated by him, sliding sideways glances his way behind reading glasses and dessert menus.

She was starting to think she was the only woman in Lexington who was immune to his good looks and casual charm. Lucky for her, she'd gotten a glimpse of the scoundrel behind the smile before succumbing to his questionable charm. She had Heath, and she had no desire to get mixed up with the likes of Jack Stillman, a confirmed ladies' man, with whom she would also be working. She was warming to the idea of him starring in Tremont's commercials—women found him irresistible, it seemed. But she still didn't trust him. The man was trouble, a rebel if she'd ever seen one, determined to have his way.

She supposed he was the same with women. Swallowing more of the dry wine, she conceded that in another place, another time, she herself might have responded to his allure, his unrefined good looks, his smooth tongue. The mere fact that she was aware of him physically, however, didn't alarm her, because knowledge was power. Subsequently, she made a pact with herself as the meal progressed to keep this man at a distance with whatever emotional tools she had handy—a sharp tongue, a cold shoulder—to preempt such an impossible situation. Who had said the best defense was a good offense? Probably some neurotic single woman afraid of losing herself to a man. Maybe Lana, after the Bill Friar incident.

"Are you sure you feel like driving?" Jack asked an hour later when they emerged from the restaurant.

"I didn't drink much more than you did," she said, giving in to her need to lean on his arm to combat her sudden lightheadedness.

"But I ate a full meal," he said. "And I outweigh you by at least a hundred pounds."

She blinked, trying to clear her head. "I'll be fine." She certainly wouldn't drive in this condition, but neither did she want Jack to take her home. She'd wait in her car until he left, then walk back into the restaurant and call a cab.

"Looks like the decision was made for you," Jack said when they approached her car, pointing to a steel device locked onto her rear wheel.

"Oh, no, they booted my car?"

"The city's new alternative to towing," he said, nodding with no apparent concern. "It's saving us thousands in tax dollars."

"Oh, shut up," she snapped, then gestured wildly. "When I pulled in, the guy leaving this spot said it was paid for for the rest of the evening." She groaned, then kicked the device, which sent pain shooting up her leg. "Ow, ow, *ow!*"

"Don't hurt yourself," he said, laughing, which only fueled her ire. While she limped in a circle, Jack pulled out a piece of paper to write down the number on the neon sticker plastered onto her window. "Looks like it's too late to call now, but you'll get it straightened out in the morning, and your car should be safe here overnight. Meanwhile, I'll take you home."

She stopped and straightened. "I...don't like motorcycles."

"Have you ever been on one?"

"No." Motorcycles were too...risky. *Jack* was too risky.

"It's just like riding with the top down on your convertible," Jack cajoled, steering her toward the bike.

Now didn't seem like the time to admit she'd only put the top down a handful of times, twice to get ficus trees home from the nursery. She lifted her index finger when an idea came to her. "I don't have a helmet."

"I have a spare," he said, unlocking a storage box behind the seat.

"But...there isn't enough room for me."

To her dismay, Jack turned her around to peruse her backside, then said, "I think we'll be able to squeeze you on board."

She continued to claim she'd rather call a taxi even as he lowered a helmet to her head. Her bun was a painful obstacle. "Ow!"

He looked amused. "Looks like you might actually have to let your hair down."

In response to his sarcasm, she withdrew two pins and released her hair, tossing it in defiance. Jack stopped suddenly and stared down at her, his expression more serious than she'd seen all evening. He was too close for her to think straight; the man emitted some sort of strange energy field—some kind of chemical, maybe? The perfume counter had reported mixed sales on the new scent that contained animal pheromones. Perhaps they should have tapped Jack Stillman instead of wrestling muskrats for the stuff.

A noisy knot of diners walked by them, breaking the spell, thank goodness. Alex was then beset with a spasm of shivers in the cool night air, although she conceded that Jack's oversize fingers fastening the chin strap of her helmet probably contributed to the gooseflesh. He slipped off his leather jacket and settled it over her shoulders. The silky lining of the heavy coat still resonated with his body heat, giving her insight as to how it might feel to be enveloped in his arms. Alex tried to drive the ludicrous thought from her mind, but his nearness set her reason on tilt, and set her skin on fire.

"Ready?"

She realized that he'd already climbed onto the machine, released the kickstand, and was waiting for her to join him.

Alex swallowed. "What do I do?"

"Left foot on this footpeg, swing right foot over the seat, then get a hand hold."

She managed all of it rather shakily, except for the hand hold. "What do I hang on to?" she asked, nearly panicked when he started the bike engine.

"Me," he tossed over this shoulder, then gunned forward, forcing her to fling her arms around his waist. "Try to enjoy it."

She tried, but she didn't. The bite of the chilly fall wind nipped at her exposed neck and hands. Traffic sounds rang in her ears. She buried her face between his shoulder blades, and the beating of his heart made her feel mortal and small—if they crashed, they'd be killed for sure. And she hadn't planned to die hanging on to a man she didn't even like.

But gradually, she did relax, and finally opened her eyes. Her senses were heightened, her pulse elevated, her awareness of the man she clung to, keen. The fuzzy warmth of security seeped into her chest—Jack wouldn't allow anything to happen to her. The vibration of the motorcycle combined with being jammed up against his body lent a heaviness to the juncture of her thighs, shocking her, but rendering her powerless to resist the sexual energy of the man and the machine. When he wheeled into her driveway and cut the engine, she was too weak to climb off without his support.

"I'll walk you up," he said gruffly, looking around the dimly lit parking lot.

She didn't protest because he seemed to have acquired a black mood since they'd left the restaurant, and appeared anxious to be rid of her. He probably thought that she was an inconvenience, or that she was a wimp about riding the bike, or that she was keeping him from a rendezvous with that redheaded tart he'd been laughing with at the bar when she arrived. Regardless, she matched his stiff gait and maintained silence until they reached her apartment door. Jack took her keys and unlocked the deadbolt, then gave her an awkward smile as he handed them back to her.

"Thanks for agreeing to meet with me," he said curtly. "I hope this project turns out to be productive for both of us."

Alex looked up, and swallowed hard. The man was gorgeous, for sure, his dark eyes nearly black in the filtered light of the hallway, his short hair appealingly rumpled from his helmet, his cheeks ruddy from the cool wind. She shrugged out of his jacket and handed it to him, self-consciously smoothing her own disheveled hair. "Thanks for the ride home. And I, too, hope this project is productive for both of us."

He didn't move, and neither did she, afraid she would

sway into the sexual pull emanating from him. Something was happening here, and although she couldn't put a finger on it, her body seemed to know. His Adam's apple moved. His mouth twitched, as if he were about to open his mouth and...and...

"Goodnight, Alex."

Say goodnight. Relief and something else less identifiable coursed through her, and she reached for the doorknob. "Goodnight, Jack." Heart thudding in her ears, Alex pushed open the door, then froze, a scream dying at the back of her throat.

"What?" He was by her side immediately.

"There!" she shrieked, cowering against him. Across the room, the silhouette of a man stood out clearly against the light pouring in from the windows.

Alex's heart jumped to her throat as Jack thrust her behind him. "Who's there?" he shouted.

The intruder didn't answer, didn't move.

"Go call the police," he barked.

She felt the muscles of his arm bunch beneath her death grip. When she realized he meant to confront the person, fear paralyzed her. He lunged across the room, tackling the dark figure. Jack's grunt reverberated through the room as both men fell to the floor. Horror descended when she heard the sound of a gunshot, and a corresponding groan from Jack.

"Jack!" she screamed. Police forgotten, she lunged for the light switch—she had to help him.

As light spilled into the room, she ran forward, then stopped at the scene before her, her hand to her open mouth. Uncontrollable laughter bubbled out, so intense she had to bend at the waist.

Jack lay sprawled facedown on top of Lana's blow-up doll Harry, who had suffered a blow*out* when he'd been tackled. Jack gingerly turned his head, blinking under the wattage of the row of track lighting running overhead, then pushed himself up, staring down at the doll's half-inflated leering face. "What the hell?"

Alex could only shake her head and laugh harder.

He frowned and lumbered to his feet, feeling his ribcage. "I'm glad you find my pain so amusing."

She sobered a tiny bit, hiding her laughter behind her fist. "Are you injured?"

One side of his mouth pulled back in a wry grin. "Just my pride."

"If it makes you feel better," Alex said, laughing anew as she walked over to the victim sagging against the floor, the life hissing out of him, "Harry got the brunt of it."

"Harry?"

"Er, Horny Harry, to be exact." She picked up the unfortunate rubber doll, glad his somewhat alarmingly anatomically correct body was covered by a pair of baggy pajamas, although his hard plastic erection was obvious beneath the thin fabric.

Jack pursed his mouth. "And does Reddinger know he has such, um, stiff competition?"

Alex threw him a withering glance. "He's not mine."

His eyebrow quirked upward. "Reddinger, or Harry here?"

He maintained a teasing expression, but she had the strangest feeling he was half-serious. "I was talking about Harry," she said lightly. "My neighbor Lana asked if she could bring some of her things over, but I didn't realize she meant him."

He emitted a low, rolling laugh. "Sounds like a lonely woman."

"It's a long story. Are you sure you're okay?" she asked as she stowed Harry safely in a chair.

He nodded. "On hindsight, I'm glad you didn't call the police."

She wet her lips, suppressing another smile. "Now I know why they call you Jack the Attack."

"Oh, now that's hilarious. And I was beginning to think you didn't have a sense of humor."

Alex warmed, realizing that in the past few hours they had gone from near-enemies to sharing a moment of laughter in her apartment.

"Nice place," he said, his head pivoting. He hesitated a second longer than necessary when his gaze passed over her bed in the far corner.

Alex ignored the zing of electricity that barbed through her. "Thanks."

"Do you live alone?" His voice held only casual curiosity.

"Yes."

"Then you play?" He nodded toward the baby grand piano.

"Not really. It was my mother's."

"Was?"

"She died a few years ago."

His brow clouded. "I'm sorry. I know how tough it is to lose a parent."

She nodded, unable to speak past the lump of emotion that lodged in her throat at his earnest tone—they did have something in common, she and this rebel.

Silence stretched between them, gazes locked, until he looked past her and gestured to the still-open door, a smile hovering on his handsome face. "Well, I guess I'd better be going."

Alex grasped the back of a bar stool and stood rigid until he walked by, closing her eyes as his energy field passed over her. At last she made her feet move, and she followed him to the door, strangely reluctant to see him leave, yet unable to identify why. "Jack."

He turned around, his hand on the doorjamb. With his

back to the light in the hallway, his face was cast in shadows.

Flustered, she gestured toward her tiny galley-style kitchen. "W-would you like a cup of coffee? It's the least I can do for someone willing to brave a prowler on my behalf." Was that her voice squeaking? Was that her heart thumping?

His dark eyes glittered and she thought he was smiling, but couldn't be sure. "You were right earlier about us keeping this relationship strictly professional," he said, "and no matter how much I'd like to stay for, um, *coffee*, I think it would seriously compromise our deal." He touched his hand to his forehead in a mock salute. "But I appreciate the offer, boss, more than you know."

Mortification bled through her veins when she realized he thought she was propositioning him. For the second time that evening, Alex banged the door shut in his face.

"AT LEAST HE KNOWS who's in charge," Lana said, forking spinach salad into her mouth.

"Believe me," Alex said, "when he called me 'boss,' it wasn't out of respect." She sneezed into her napkin. "And that damn motorcycle ride gave me a cold. Yesterday was the first sick day I've taken since I had mono when I was eighteen."

"Didn't Jeff Summers have mono about that same time?"

Alex frowned. "So?"

"Ah, so your *last* hell-raising boyfriend made you sick, too."

"Jack Stillman is *not* my boyfriend, Lana. I'm engaged for heaven's sake!" Then she pursed her mouth. "But now that you mention it, he does remind me of Jeff—what a loser he turned out to be."

"So either bad boys are gritty and germ-laden, or they wear down your resistance," Lana teased.

Feeling sour, Alex severed a miniloaf of bread with a small serrated knife then set it back down on the restaurant table. Jack Stillman's words from two nights ago still rang in her ears. "How that man interpreted 'would you like a cup of coffee?' to mean 'would you like to have sex with me?' I'm not sure, but it's indicative of his gutter mind and abounding arrogance."

"Maybe you were giving off signals," Lana said with a shrug.

"That's ridiculous."

Her friend eyed her. "You don't find him attractive?"

She averted her eyes. "Well...I'm not blind. He's nice looking, as much as I can remember." She'd recalled every contour of his face, every expression, at the oddest times over the past couple of days.

"You're blushing."

"I am not."

Her friend laughed. "You know, Alex, the rest of the world entertains a naughty thought once in a while and even *survives.* Lighten up. It's okay to lust after this guy."

Alex scoffed. "Lana, I'm in love with Heath. We're getting married, remember?"

Lana leveled her violet eyes across the table. "So you've set a date?"

She squirmed on the tiny chair. "Not yet, but soon."

After a few seconds of pregnant silence, Lana said, "I just hope you're not settling for Heath because you think it's the right thing to do."

She sighed, a little annoyed with the psychoanalysis. "What's that supposed to mean?"

Lana put down her fork. "Alex, I know you. You miss your mother, and your father is so...distant, it's natural that you would turn to Heath for the security of a warm, fuzzy family."

Alex swallowed the lump of emotion that had formed in her throat. "What's wrong with wanting security and a family?"

"Not a thing. As long as you truly love the man."

"But I do love Heath."

A dreamy expression came over her friend's face. "But does he make you feel *passionate* and *alive?*"

She attempted a laugh. "Lana, passion isn't the glue of a lasting relationship. You were passionate about Bill Friar, and look what a mistake it would have been to marry *him.*"

Lana held up her hand, stop-sign fashion. "Right you are. I'll keep my mouth shut."

"Good," Alex said with a smile. Her friend resumed eating, unaware that her words had dredged up worries Alex thought she'd put to rest when Heath had proposed.

Suddenly her friend burst out laughing. "I just wish I'd been there when Jack tackled Harry—oh, that's hysterical." She dabbed at her eyes with her napkin.

Glad for the change in subject, Alex smiled wickedly at the memory of the great Jack humbled. "It was a bright moment in my week. Is Harry repairable?"

"He blew a nut, but with a little duct tape, he'll be as good as new. I'm not sure why men need two of those things anyway. By the way, when will you see your hero again?"

She frowned, uncomfortable talking about Jack Stillman on the heels of discussing her wedding. "We're meeting in less than an hour to select his wardrobe for the commercial shoot."

"Oooh, dressing and undressing—sounds like fun to me."

"Fun? We'll be lucky to find something big enough to accommodate his ego."

Lana wagged her eyebrows. "Do you need an assistant?"

Alex pointed her pinkie across the café table. "It's shameless women like you who keep shameless men like Jack Stillman on a pedestal."

"Yeah, well, it's uptight women like you who keep Metamucil on the shelf."

"I'm trying to be professional about this."

"And it sounds to me like he's abiding by your wishes. After all, he could've stayed for coffee the other night and not have respected you the next morning."

"I offered the man a lousy cup of coffee, and that's *all.*"

Lana laughed. "Don't worry, I believe you. You're the

only woman I can think of who wouldn't jump his bones at the first chance."

"Why does that sound like an insult?"

"Because you're being way too sensitive. Not to change the subject, but what's the status of your promotion to vice president?"

"Status quo. A decision should be announced any day now."

"I'll keep my fingers crossed for you."

"Thanks."

Lana glanced at her watch. "I hate to run, but I'm meeting with the bank manager this afternoon."

Alex clasped her hands together. "You're buying the coffee shop!"

"*Thinking* about it, that's all."

She grinned, elated for her friend. "Let me know if you need a silent partner."

Lana's bordeaux-colored mouth quirked from side to side. "Thanks, Alex, but I'd rather have your friendship than your money."

"It doesn't have to be an either-or situation—look at me and my dad."

Lana gave her a pointed look.

Alex sighed in concession. "Okay. Just let me know if I can help."

"Thanks. And eyes wide open this afternoon in the dressing room—I expect *firm* details."

"Get out of here."

"Bye."

Alex toyed with the angel hair pasta on her plate a few minutes longer before she abandoned her lunch, troubling thoughts niggling the back of her mind. She'd been outraged at Jack's recognition that she was physically attracted to him, and it was that outrage which had kept her awake at night, she told herself, not the image of his mocking grin, his dancing eyes.

And this infuriating anticipation of seeing Jack again was only because she wanted to get the whole thing over with, this expensive, time-consuming experiment of her father's. And the dressing and undressing part was nothing to be nervous about—she'd worked with plenty of male models. One thing was certain: She would have to take control of the situation early on to maintain the upper hand where Jack Stillman was concerned.

Yes, she decided, reaching for her water glass with a shaky hand, *take control.*

CONSIDERING THE WAY their business-dinner meeting had ended, Jack figured he'd better arrive at the wardrobe meeting at Tremont's early. But as luck would have it, Stripling had questions regarding some of Jack's entertainment expenses incurred the previous year. Since Jack could barely recall the events of the previous *week,* he had problems substantiating the receipts. Jack spent over an hour trying to convince the man that The Golden Pony was a hotbed of business networking opportunities—this while ignoring Tuesday's muttered quotes from the Bible on the evils of the flesh as she flitted around the office taking measurements. For what purpose the woman was measuring, he didn't care to know.

In short, he was late.

"You're late," Alex confirmed when she emerged from her office to meet him, her arms crossed, her red mouth unsmiling.

"Sorry," he said, shaken anew by her beauty. "Problems at the office."

"*Your* problems, not mine. Let's go—my time is money."

And his wasn't, apparently. How did she do that? he wondered. How did she give the impression she was snapping her fingers in time to her rapid little stride. He had to jog to catch up to her, barely making it onto the elevator before the door closed. Sensing her mood, he stepped to the opposite side of the small cubicle and whistled tunelessly while they descended. Not a great lover of perfumes—he refused to stray from Old Spice—he nonetheless appreciated the citrusy fragrance emanating from her rigid body. Very...tasty.

Her hair was tightly bound again. She wore an immaculate pale gray suit with sharp, uncluttered lines and a lemon-yellow blouse peeking through the vee of her buttoned jacket. He'd bet the woman didn't own a single garment with polka dots or ruffles. Ten to one, she slept in that big cold-looking bed of hers in black flannel pajamas with thick socks on her feet. Reddinger didn't seem to be the hot-blooded type.

As if she were reading his mind, her shoulders shook with a shiver as she stared straight ahead.

"Are you cold?"

She sniffed. "I caught pneumonia riding on that death machine of yours the other night."

"Oh, good," he said as the doors slid open. "Something else today that's my fault." He swept his arm toward the opening and gave her a pleasant smile.

Her mouth tightened and she strode out into the men's department as if she owned it. Which she kind of *did*, he acknowledged with a smirk, then followed her, wishing he'd taken more pains dressing this morning. His "proper" attire was negligible to begin with, and the set of barbells in the corner of the Florida guest house he'd shared with Teresa—or was it Tammy?—had expanded his biceps and deltoids to the seams of the polo shirts in his closet. One beige golf shirt had been a passable fit, so he'd tucked it into navy slacks, which weren't bad. But he couldn't find a belt or a pair of non-holey socks, so he skipped both and donned a pair of buttery-soft loafers, which had once been tan-colored, if memory served.

Oh, well, clothes had never been that important to him. Nakedness was just so much more interesting.

"Hi, Reggie," Alex said as she walked up to a sales counter.

He recognized the handsome black youth immediately because of the resemblance of his smile to Tuesday's.

"Hello, Ms. Tremont."

"Mr. Stillman, this is Reggie Humphrey, one of our top sales associates. Reggie, this is—"

"Jack Stillman," Reggie finished, stepping out from behind the counter and extending his hand with a grin. "This is a real pleasure, sir, working with Jack the Attack."

"The pleasure's mine," he said smoothly.

Alex cleared her throat, bouncing a time's-a-wasting glance between them. "Let's get started, shall we? Reggie, would you fetch a tailor?"

The young man nodded, then disappeared. Alex turned back to him and tapped the notepad she held. "I'll need your sizes, please."

She really was a stunner, he affirmed as he studied her smooth skin, and her luminous eyes, which were aimed straight at him. Darn his promise to Derek—he bet she was a real tigress in bed. Sometimes the bun-packing yuppies were sleepers. "Sizes of which body parts?" He grinned, hoping to cajole a smile out of her.

Instead, her mouth pursed into a tight little bow and fifteen seconds passed before she said through gritted teeth, "Shoulders."

"Forty-four."

She made a note with a gold-tone pen. "Height?"

"Six-three."

"Neck?"

"Sixteen and a half."

"Sleeve?"

"Thirty-six."

"Waist?"

"Same."

"Shoe size?"

"Thirteen, extra wide."

She shook her head, as if disgusted.

"It has its advantages," he felt compelled to inform Miss Unenlightened.

When she glanced up, pink tinged her cheeks, much to his satisfaction. She closed her eyes briefly, then looked back to the notepad. "Inseam?"

"Thirty-six."

Reggie returned, reporting that a tailor would meet them at the dressing rooms.

"Thank you, Reggie. I need you to record the items of clothing as I select them."

Jack squirmed. As *she* selected them?

Reggie produced a rolling clothes rack, and appeared poised to follow her around.

She walked to the suits first, walking her fingers through them. "The brown Twain, the light blue Dion, the olive Tremont's." Alex moved from rack to rack, rattling off colors and labels for slacks, shirts, ties, sweaters, jeans, belts, socks, underwear, shoes and a couple of items he'd never even heard of, all of it conservative and stuffy. She frequently consulted Reggie, whose opinion she seemed to respect.

"Follow me," she said, explaining that a couple of dressing rooms had been set aside for the fitting. He and Reggie traipsed behind her as if carrying the ends of her fur-trimmed robe. Jack did, however, manage to snag a package from an underwear rack as he trotted by. If he had to be subjected to this dress up game, why not shake up Alex a teensy bit?

The dressing room area was a secluded clearing of gleaming gray marble. A love seat faced two changing stalls with louvered three-quarter doors. Jack suspected that special male customers were treated to this private alcove during extensive shopping trips. Alex directed Reggie where to place the rolling clothes rack, then thanked and dismissed him.

Alex consulted the list Reggie had assembled, then without ceremony, transferred a stack of clothing from the rack to his arms. "We'll start with underwear so the tailor can take your precise measurements."

"You don't trust the ones I gave you?"

Her smile was deceptively sweet. "Men have a way of exaggerating in one direction or the other."

He lifted his eyebrows, but her expression was threatening, as if she dared him to make a smart remark. Amused by her solemn demeanor, Jack simply smiled and moved obediently into the dressing room. The louvered door covered him from shoulders to knees, allowing him to watch Alex watch him beneath her lashes as he removed his shirt. Masculine pride welled in his chest as he tossed his shirt on a bench. Twenty-two was a distant memory, but thanks to good genes and occasional exercise, he'd been able to maintain a decent physique.

"Did you get your car released?" he asked.

She sneezed into a handkerchief, then nodded. "Yes, in exchange for ninety-five dollars."

He whistled low. "You should have let me buy your dinner." When she didn't answer, he added, "Next time." Again, she didn't answer. Shrugging, Jack removed the black thong underwear from the package he'd nabbed and proceeded to stuff himself into the scrap of Lycra. Damn, men actually wore these things? A jock strap was more comfortable. After much adjusting, he stepped back to appraise his bulging reflection. Not half bad for a has-been.

He glanced over the door to where Alex sat in the middle

of the love seat, legs crossed primly, expression humorless. "Mr. Stillman, I don't have all day, and you still have a lot of clothes to try on."

Incredibly, his body leapt at the sound of her chiding voice—he'd never been turned on before by a scolding. He sucked in a breath through his teeth and said, "Coming." Chuckling at his own word choice, he stepped out, adopting a most innocent look on his face.

AT THE SOUND OF THE DOOR clicking open, Alex looked up...and the pen slipped out of her suddenly loose hand. At first glance, she feared he was naked, then realized with no small amount of relief that his privates were covered by a minuscule amount of stretchy black fabric. He stood before her, hands on hips, legs shoulder-width apart. His bronze body was finely corded and accented with patches of dark hair on his chest, stomach and thighs. He had the physique of an athlete, all right—any athlete. Long-limbed and so finely put together, his body seemed tuned for any type of physical activity. Sexual awareness zipped through her, warming her erogenous zones.

At last, she dragged her gaze from him and pretended to study the list Reggie had assembled. "I...don't recall seeing that particular...garment...on the list." Was that her voice, high and breathless?

"They were on the pile," he said simply. His shrug displaced all kinds of muscle. "This modeling stuff is new to me—am I supposed to turn around or something?"

On treacherous ground, Alex swallowed, striving to calm her jumping pulse, the desire that had pooled low in her stomach. Perhaps if she didn't have to look him in the eye... "That...would be fine."

He turned to stand with his back to her, his legs wide apart. The skinny strap of the thong left nothing to the imagination, and why should it, she asked herself, when the reality was so impressive? The sole flaw on his body, if it could be called a flaw, was a black tattoo high on his right shoulder, a pair of wings about the size of a silver dollar. The lower regions of her body thrummed outrageously at the sight of those wings, given movement and texture by the bumpy muscle beneath his smooth skin.

"You...can turn back around now," she said, struggling for composure. In hindsight, she should have started with suits. Where the devil was that tailor?

He didn't move, except to lift a hand to scratch his temple. "Gee, boss, I don't think turning around would be such a great idea at the moment."

The meaning of his words sunk in, sending heat to her thighs. Then she heard footsteps on the other side of the privacy screen and breathed a sigh of relief that the tailor had arrived.

"Hello, my dear—oh!"

Alex turned just in time to see her father's eyes widen as his gaze landed on nearly nude Jack. Worse, Heath walked in behind her father and adopted a similar expression. Her heart jumped to her throat and she jumped to her feet when she realized how compromising the situation looked. "Father, Heath—what an unexpected surprise." She hugged the clipboard to her chest and pasted on a serious expression.

Jack looked over his shoulder and lifted his hand in greeting, but otherwise didn't move a muscle. "How's it going, Mr. T? Reddinger?"

"Fine, Jack," her father said, his voice laced with amusement as he gave her a questioning look. Heath just continued to look from her to Jack. Or rather, from her to Jack's backside.

Wanting to disappear, she instead conjured up a sublime smile for Heath. "Wh-when did you get back in town?"

"Not long ago," he replied absently.

"And not soon enough," her father muttered for her ears only.

She frowned at him and shook her head in warning.

"Heath and I were both looking for you, my dear," her father said in a louder voice. "Tess told us where to find you."

She was going to fire that woman. "Jack and I were just starting to choose his wardrobe for the photo shoot and the commercial."

"Let's try to keep the censors off our back, shall we?" Al said cheerfully.

"Father," she said, exasperated. "We're waiting for the tailor."

"When he gets here," her father said, peering around Jack, then clapping him on the back, "let him know our boy is a left-handed dresser."

Alex closed her eyes briefly, her cheeks flaming.

"Alex," Heath said. "May I see you outside?"

"Of course," she said, unreasonably nervous, but delighted for an excuse to flee the preposterous scene.

Once they stepped around the corner, Heath scanned the area, then grabbed her hand, pulled her into an alcove, and kissed her soundly. Surprised at his uncharacteristic behavior at work, Alex laughed and drew back, hiding her unexplainable irritation. "What's this all about?"

"I missed you," he said, his gaze intent. "And I guess it did something to me when I saw you with a half-dressed man."

She scoffed, feeling prickly. "That's ridiculous. I can barely stand the man."

"Good," he said, giving her a crooked grin. "I'm sorry I missed our dinner at Gerrard's."

Alex fidgeted, reluctant to admit she'd used their reservation, even sat at their *table*, with the man she could barely stand. Heath wouldn't understand the circumstances, she reasoned—Jack giving her a ride home, then tackling a

would-be attacker in her apartment. It all sounded too...
intimate.

Anxious to spend time with Heath and erase the memory
of Jack, she smoothed his jacket lapel and tilted her face up
at him. "How about us taking the afternoon off tomorrow
and using my father's box at Keeneland for opening day at
the races?"

Heath smiled. "Terrific. I'll pick you up at your apartment
at noon."

Alex exhaled in relief—just the two of them. By the time
she got through this disconcerting afternoon, she'd be ready
for a day without the presence of "Jack the Attack" Stillman.

"WHEW," Jack said to Reggie upon emerging from the
dressing room. "Am I ever glad *that* is over." The binding
thong had been nothing compared to the torture of behav-
ing himself around Alex all afternoon while she pulled and
poked at his clothing, suggesting alterations that the tailor
marked with a gazillion little razor-sharp pins. "That tailor
missed his calling in acupuncture."

Reggie laughed good-naturedly. "When my mom told
me you were going to be the new spokesman for Tremont's,
I was hoping I'd have the chance to work with you, sir."

"Call me Jack. 'Sir' makes me feel like I'm a hundred
years old." Jack leaned one arm on the counter. "Listen,
Reggie, speaking of your mother, is she, uh—"

"Unstable?" the young man asked with a grin.

"Well, the thought had crossed my mind."

"To be honest, all of us kids have just gotten used to her
eccentricity. She travels around the country, stays with one
of us for a while, then moves on to another."

"How many siblings do you have?"

"Nine."

"Wow. No wonder she acts like a general."

"Yep, she's a go-getter. If it makes you feel any better, though, she's a smart lady."

"Yeah, well, no offense, but I think I have too many smart ladies in my life right now." He looked around.

"Ms. Tremont left."

"Probably went to let the air out of my tires," he muttered.

Reggie laughed. "She said she was going to accessories to buy a new hat for tomorrow."

"Tomorrow?"

"Opening day at Keeneland. Said she and Mr. Reddinger are using her father's box seats."

Jack always wondered who sat in the expensive box seats, and now he knew. Personally, he thought the cheap seats had the best access to the betting windows, but then again, the people in the boxes attended the horse races mostly to socialize, to see and be seen, not to wager their beer money on the trifecta.

"Sounds fun, doesn't it?" Reggie asked, his voice wistful.

"It'll probably rain," Jack said sourly, then thanked Reggie for his help and moved toward the escalator. He wasn't sure why the thought of Alex spending the day with Reddinger bothered him so much—they were a couple before he came on the scene and probably would be long after his stint with Tremont's ended. Nursing an increasing bad mood, he stepped onto the down escalator only to see Al Tremont on the opposite escalator, being carried up.

"Jack, I was hoping you hadn't left," the beaming man called, turning as they passed. "I forgot to ask you earlier if you would join me tomorrow in my box at Keeneland for opening day."

Jack's ill humor vanished. He cupped his hands around his mouth so his voice would travel across the distance widening between them. "Thanks—I'll be there!"

TUESDAY WAGGED HER FINGER. "With work coming out of your big ears, you're going to spend the afternoon at the racetrack?"

"It's business," Jack insisted.

"So if your brother calls, I can tell him where you are?"

He balked. "That might not be prudent."

She put one hand on her hip, arm akimbo, and nodded. "Mmm-hmm. I thought so."

Jack gave her his most charming grin. "But I feel lucky. In fact, I'm planning to win enough money to get new equipment for the office." He gestured around, then stopped and squinted. Several vines and ferns, plus two palm trees accented shelves and corners in the front office. "Where did all the plants come from?"

"I have a green thumb," she said, then handed him a stack of papers. "Sign, lick and mail."

"Tuesday." Jack ran his hand down the length of his face. "There is no job! I can't pay you for working here."

"Five dollars," she said, pulling out a file drawer. Rows of new color-coded hanging files swayed gently.

"What?"

"Put five dollars on the daily double for me, horses two and five." She turned a placid smile in his direction. "And that'll be my pay for the first two weeks."

"What if it doesn't come in?"

She shrugged. "Life is a gamble."

Jack pursed his mouth—he could live with that. He

walked through the doorway into the back office where the auditor still claimed Derek's desk. "How's it going, Mr. Stripling?"

The man scowled. "If you must know, terribly." His voice and hands were shaking, and the boardlike device was still strapped to his back by a cord around his waist and chest.

Jack poured himself a cup of coffee from the little refreshment center Tuesday had established on a sturdy table she'd confiscated from the supply room—coffeemaker, tea bags, creamer, sugar and fresh minibagels every morning. He'd considered hinting for jelly donuts, but decided not to push his luck. Her one rule had been not to touch the single china cup and saucer sitting nearby—it had been her mother's and was to be used only in emergencies, she instructed. Jack wasn't exactly sure what kind of an emergency would require fine china, but he hadn't argued. He lifted his mug in the other man's direction. "More receipt problems?"

"No, not more receipt problems," the man snapped. "Unbeknownst to me, your office manager has been plying my tea with some repulsive concoction of dried leaves—she's probably trying to poison me."

"Tuesday," Jack yelled, stirring cream into his coffee. "Are you trying to poison Mr. Stripling?"

"No," she yelled back.

Jack took a bite out of a blueberry bagel and shrugged. "You heard her."

Stripling's face reddened to a deep crimson. "I'm on the verge of convulsions here."

Tuesday appeared and sashayed by, rolling her eyes as she headed toward the bathroom. "It's called energy, tax man. That's what ginseng does for a body."

Jack dropped into his chair, chewing. When the door closed behind her, he said, "So that's what she's on."

"*Mr.* Stillman," Stripling croaked, his eyes bulging. "This will not look good in my report."

"Yeah, well, life's a bitch." Jack unfolded the paper and snapped it open to the day's racing form. "You play the ponies?"

"I most certainly do not."

He made a sympathetic sound. "Too bad. Races five and eight have great-looking long shots."

After a stretch of silence, Mr. Stripling cleared his throat, then offered, "My father was a groom for Spectacular Wish."

He flicked down the corner of the paper. "No kidding?"

The little man shifted in his chair, his expression slightly less unpleasant. "I do not kid."

"Then you *have* to place a bet, because the third horse in the eighth race is the granddaughter of Spectacular Wish."

He had the man's attention. "Through mare or sire?"

"Sire."

"Maiden race?"

"Yep."

"What are the odds?"

"Sixty to one."

"Let me see that form," the man said, and stood up with amazing agility for a man bound to a board.

"LOVELY HAT," Heath said with a smile.

Alex touched the wide brim of her chocolate-colored straw hat. "You don't think it's too big?"

"No. I think it's very chic."

"We're pushing these for fall, so I thought I'd advertise." She stepped back to allow him inside her apartment. "You look nice yourself."

He wore classic horseman colors: hunter green slacks and a tan shirt, with a navy-and-green-plaid cotton sweater tied around his neck. "Thanks," he said, looking boyish as he gave the bridge of his small glasses a nudge.

"Just give me a minute to change my purse." Alex agonized between two purses, finally settling on a brown leather tote to go with her cream-colored water-silk dress, fitted through the torso, but with a long flowing skirt. At the last minute, she tossed a brown leopard-print scarf around her shoulders.

"Jacket?" Heath asked.

"No, I—" Alex looked up and stopped, staring at the black leather coat Heath held by the collar. *Jack's* coat. Oh, no. "Wh-where did you find that?" she asked, stalling.

Mouth pursed, he nodded to a table behind the door. "Under there."

"Really? It…must be one of the things Lana dropped off." She smiled wide—convincingly, she hoped.

"It's a man's coat."

Her smile dissolved. "Well, she's been stealing things lately—it's all very weird." Alex looked at her watch and gasped. "Oh, fudge. Look. We'd better get going if we don't want to miss the first race." With one motion, Alex yanked the coat out of his hand and tossed it over a chair. "You know how bad parking can be." She steered Heath back into the hallway and closed the door behind her.

And Heath, bless his trusting heart, didn't ask another question about the jacket. Just to make sure, she chattered the entire drive about news and nonsense, since all the work-related topics that came to mind seemed to lead back to Jack: The vacated vice presidency…proving herself by taking on difficult tasks…the Jack Stillman project. Sliding sales…a new ad campaign…the Jack Stillman project.

"It's crowded all right," Heath noted as they waited in a long line of cars to access the preferred parking area. "I'll drop you off, then park and meet you at our seats."

"Okay," she agreed, feeling a bit guilty. She didn't mind the walk, but she did want to minimize the chance of the mysterious leather jacket coming up again. Once inside, the crowd noise and the excitement would alleviate conversation for the most part. She gave him a loving smile before she alighted and closed the door to his black Mercedes. As he pulled away, Alex berated herself for not simply telling Heath the truth. After all, her evening with Jack had been purely innocent, hadn't it?

Hadn't it?

She sighed inwardly as she merged with the crowd of people moving through the admission gates. The Keeneland facility was a rambling two-story stone structure that housed covered walkways, spectator grandstands, restaurants, and window after window for placing bets. Horse racing appealed to all walks of life—retirees looking for a day of inexpensive entertainment, college kids looking for an excuse to party, professionals looking for a network, dyed-in-the-wool horse people looking for a reputation, and hard-core gamblers looking for this month's rent. Most people dressed up, and many women wore hats, as was tradition. As far as people-watching venues were concerned, Keeneland was one of the finest.

Alex loved it here. Just walking past the paddock area where the horses exercised was thrilling—the sight of the colorful silks, the pungent odor of groomed horseflesh, the whinnying of eager mounts. All of it sent the blood rushing through her veins, as if she were a teensy part of the centuries-old legacy.

But the best moment came after climbing the stairs to the stands and walking out for the first breathless view of the track. Awesome. The enormous ring of freshly raked black earth was lined with a fence on both sides, and skirted by lush grass and beautifully manicured shrubbery that spelled out "Keeneland" in enormous letters. As large as a movie screen, the black tote board sat on the inner ring of grass, already flashing jockey changes and entry scratches. The entire scene hummed and was poignant enough to make a person want to burst out singing "My Old Kentucky Home."

Her spirits lifted with every step as she made her way toward the box seats in the milling crowd. Alex held on to her hat and tilted her face to the sun—she was spending a gorgeous day with the man who cared most about her, and Jack Stillman was far, far away.

"Well, if it isn't a small world."

Alex froze, unwilling to believe the familiar voice behind her belonged to the person she thought it did.

"I said, *if it isn't a small world.*"

Keeping a firm hold on her hat, Alex whirled. She gaped at Jack Stillman lounging in her father's box, clad in faded jeans and a pale blue denim shirt, with his black booted feet crossed at the ankles and propped on the little half wall that separated their four seats from the adjacent box. Small binoculars hung around his neck.

She marched closer and gasped, "What are you doing here?"

"Drinking a beer," he said, lifting the half-empty plastic cup.

"I mean, what are you doing *here,* in our box?"

He grinned behind black sunglasses. "Your dad invited me."

Her heart pounded at the thought of sharing such a small space with him and—good Lord—with him *and* Heath for several hours. "Why?"

Unfazed by her obvious disapproval, he shrugged. "Because he likes me, I suppose."

Exasperated, she closed her eyes and took a deep breath. "Where *is* my father?"

"I haven't seen him, he told me to meet him here." He peered around her. "Is your boyfriend with you?"

Alex gritted her teeth, then said, "Yes, Heath is with me, and this seating arrangement simply will not work."

"Why not?" He looked at the chair wedged next to his and the two close behind him. "Four seats, four people." He lifted his sunglasses and squinted up at her. "You might have to lose that lampshade on your head, though."

Her mouth fell open. "You insufferable—"

Jack stood abruptly, balancing his beer with one hand, waving with the other. "Hey, Mr. T!"

Alex blew out a long, shaky breath, fisting her hands to resist strangling Jack, then turned to offer her father a welcoming smile.

"Jack! And Alex—what a delightful surprise!"

She leaned forward to kiss her father's cheek, but her hat poked him in the eye.

"Goodness, my dear, that thing is dangerous."

"I'm sorry," she murmured, shooting a murderous look toward Jack who hid his smile behind a drink from his cup. "I should have asked if you were using the box today. With Gloria the Gold—" She stopped, bit her tongue, then continued, "I mean, with Gloria out of town, I just assumed it would be okay if Heath and I came."

"But it is," her father said cheerfully. "This is a family box, Alex, you know that. We'll have a wonderful time, all of us." He put one arm around her shoulders, and one arm around Jack's, pulling them into him. "And with Jack being our company spokesman, he's practically family."

JACK GRINNED AT AL—the man was immensely likable. And he respected him for his down-to-earth attitude despite his accomplishments and wealth. He realized suddenly how this man and his own father had formed a bond during their brief encounter. Paul Stillman, like Jack, would have responded to Al Tremont's magnanimous outlook, and Al surely reacted to his father's spirit of generosity. In fact, Al reminded him a bit of his father—not so much in looks as in personality. The kinship was comforting.

He glanced from Al's glowing face to Alex, who glared at him beneath the brim of her ridiculous hat with an almost palpable dislike. Did he imagine it, or did she pull closer to her father? Puzzled, Jack withdrew from Al's casual embrace, and excused himself to collect drinks for the group. While standing in line at the concession stand on the top level, he mulled his observation. Was it possible that Alex was *jealous* of her father's time and attention?

From his vantage point behind and above the stands, he watched Alex with her father, studying their body language. They were still standing, as was most of the crowd since thirty minutes remained until the first race. Alex seemed to find excuses to touch him—straightening the collar of his golf shirt, reaching up to smooth a strand of his sparse white hair.

Al appeared to tolerate her ministrations, but not much more. In fact, he seemed more absorbed in his racing form than in the elegant woman next to him who so obviously adored him. Jack frowned as Reddinger emerged from the crowd to join them. Al shook his hand, but kept Reddinger at arm's length. The man leaned close to Alex and angled his head as if to kiss her, but the hat got in the way.

Jack smiled.

He paid for four beers and four bowls of thick, dark burgoo stew, then elbowed his way back to the seats. "Lunch is served," he said, nodding hello to Reddinger, who nodded back with a distinctly unfriendly look.

"Ahh," Al Tremont said. "I've been craving burgoo since I last had it at the spring races." He collected a bowl and a cup of beer, then settled into one of the two front chairs. Jack looked back and forth between the happy couple. "There's enough here for everyone, and my arms are getting a little tired."

"Um, we don't eat red meat," Reddinger said, wrinkling his nose as his hand snaked around Alex's waist. The man looked like a prep school class president. He probably owned a pink sport coat.

"More for us," Al chirped, having already put a dent in his first portion of the stew thick with a dozen kinds of meat, including wild game.

Jack smiled back at Reddinger and Alex, then nodded toward the beer. "Do you beatniks eat hops and barley?"

"Actually, we prefer mint juleps," Reddinger said.

Naturally.

"Ah, have a beer," Al said, waving away their resistance. "You two don't know how to have a good time."

Jack struggled to hide his mirth as the pair frowned, then dutifully retrieved their cups of beer. He started to claim the seat next to Al, but the older man held up his hand.

"Jack, I need to discuss a few matters with Heath. Would you mind if he sat with me?"

"Not at all, sir." He exchanged tight smiles with Alex and Reddinger, then dropped into the seat behind Al and proceeded to eat. The couple stood around, shifting from foot to foot and murmuring for a couple of minutes before Reddinger sat down next to Al. Within a few minutes, the men had their heads together.

Alex stood a few steps away in the grandstand aisle, apparently unaware that the sun turned the thin dress she wore into a virtual peep show. Jack settled back in his chair to enjoy the view of her slender silhouette, the curve of her breasts bound up in a thin-strapped bra, the line of her hip skimmed by high-cut panties. Damn, with her long graceful neck and delicate limbs, the woman could easily be mistaken for a ballet dancer instead of a ball-buster. He took a long sip of cool beer and swallowed hard.

"Jack, we're going to place our bets," Al said, standing. "Want to come?"

Jack tore his gaze from Alex. "No, thanks, I'm covered for the first two races."

"Alex?"

She shook her head, and with the shade of her huge hat, nearly caused an eclipse of the sun. "I'd rather not fight the crowd."

"I'll place a bet for you," Heath said, and she smiled her thanks.

Jack frowned as the men turned and climbed up the concrete steps toward the covered top level where most of the betting windows were located. As much as Jack wanted to keep ogling her, he was even more compelled to bring her closer. "You going to stand all day?"

The only indication that she'd heard him was a slight lift of her chin. Then, holding the cup of beer as if it were swill, she stepped inside the box, moved her folding padded chair as far away from Jack's as possible—a full two inches—and sat down primly.

Jack watched with his tongue in his cheek as she looked for a place to set her unwieldy shoulder bag and a place to position her expensively clad feet. After a few minutes of shifting, adjusting, and fidgeting, she fell still, staring straight ahead, her shoulders shoved back against the metal chair.

"Comfortable?" he asked.

She turned her head and the brim of her hat poked him in the eye.

"Ow!"

"I'm sorry," she said, jerking back and spilling most of her beer on her dress. "Oh, dammit!" She jumped up and held the wet fabric of her skirt away from her. With his lap full of unclaimed food, Jack could only lean forward and dab at the wetness on her thigh with a handful of napkins.

"Stop it!" she snapped, swatting at his hand. When she realized that people around them were staring, she sat down, morosely holding the half-full cup of beer.

"Why don't you drink it before you drown yourself?"

She shot him a sideways glare, then lifted the cup to her tight little mouth and took a tentative sip. "You left your coat at my apartment," she said, her voice accusing.

"I figured as much," he said. "I kept forgetting to ask if you found it."

"*Heath* found it."

"Oh." He smiled into his beer, then spooned in the last mouthful of burgoo and chewed slowly. "Got you in trouble, did I?"

"No!" She turned her head and her hat poked him in the eye again.

"Ow!" Jack covered his watery eye and glowered at her with the other one.

She winced. "I'm sorry!"

Jack set down his trash, then politely said, "Excuse me." He stood and with both hands, lifted the hat from her dark head and flung it across the top of the crowd down toward the infield, where the more rowdy patrons gathered in a sea of moving color.

"Hey!" she shouted, staring open-mouthed as the hat sailed on the air like a big, brown Frisbee, finally hooking onto the head of a humongous man, who promptly ripped it off and winged it farther down the line, like a beach ball in a sports stadium.

Her eyes widened to dangerous proportions, and her face flushed fuchsia. Sputtering, she glared at Jack. "That hat cost three hundred dollars!"

He whistled low as he settled back in his chair and retrieved his beer. "Looks like you're going to have to win big today to recoup that loss."

"Me? You mean *you!*" She stood and stared down at him until he'd taken two more deep drinks of beer. Her arms, shoulders, and fisted hands began to shake. "I...you...I'm going to tell—"

"Your daddy? Or your boyfriend?" he asked, half expecting the woman to tackle him, and fully expecting to like it.

"You are so immature," she hissed.

"Mr. Stillman?"

Jack turned to see a red-haired man standing near him, holding an impressive looking camera and wearing what looked to be some kind of press pass. "Yes?"

"My name is Majeris—I'm the sports anchor for the local PBC affiliate. Sammy Richardson told me to look you up while I was here covering opening day. Said you'd just signed on as a spokesman for a local business, and that I might get a sound bite for tonight's broadcast."

Jack rose and extended his hand. "Nice to meet you."

"Pleasure's mine, sir. You're a legend around the sports desk."

Smiling, Jack said, "That's nice to hear, especially since I've been out of the game for so long. But I'm back in town, running an advertising firm with my brother, Derek—he also played football for UK—and there's a possibility I might become the spokesman for Tremont's department store." He grinned and extended his arm to include Alex, who, besides wearing a dazed expression, sported a wet, stained dress and hat-flattened hair. "Meet my lovely boss, Ms. Alexandria Tremont."

Majeris lifted his camera and shot a half-dozen pictures of the two of them before Alex could even blink.

11

ALEX FINALLY RECOVERED enough to ask the reporter, "Excuse me, but who did you say told you about Mr. Stillman?" Tremont's had not yet issued a press release announcing the name of their new spokesman—Alex had wanted to wait until the end of the two weeks, in the highly likely event that Jack would not work out.

"Sammy Richardson."

"Sammy is producing the commercial spots," Jack supplied. "We spoke this morning to set up studio time for Monday. I figured the station would be sending out someone to cover opening race day, so I thought why not get a headstart on publicity?"

She manufactured a smile, thinking that throwing Jack under the pounding hooves of the horses as they raced by would surely make the eleven o'clock news. "Yes, why not?" she parroted, finger combing her hair in an attempt to counter the effects of her now-missing hat. "Mr. Majeris, you may report a *rumor* that Jack Stillman will be signed by Tremont's, but our public relations department will supply your station with a press release in due time."

The man nodded curtly. "A couple more pictures, Jack?" He shot Alex a guilty glance, then added, "Of Jack alone?"

Tingling with indignance, Alex stepped back while the young man shot several photos in succession with Jack grinning into the lens. Then Jack signed an autograph for the young man who asked that he sign "Jack the Attack." And either several spectators had already recognized Jack or the reporter's camera had tipped them off, because before Majeris could leave, a knot of people had gathered for autographs. He worked the crowd like a pro, flirting and signing his name with a flourish.

Alex drained her half cup of beer, then sat down when the alcohol bypassed her empty stomach and zoomed straight to her head. He was a good-looking man, she admitted miserably, an opinion that was mirrored in the eyes of the women trying to get close to him. The denim shirt he wore accentuated his dark hair and his ruggedness. But she remembered too well that he looked just as good in a designer suit. And even better in black thong underwear. Extremely vexed, she acknowledged that her father's choice to make Jack the store spokesman might not have been as faulty as she had first presumed.

God, how she hated being wrong. And in front of her father, no less.

By the time his fan club had dissipated, Alex had even ventured to taste a spoonful of the dark stew he had bought—which wasn't half bad—and she was contemplating going to the ladies room to remove her pale, sheer panty hose. Why keep up the pretense of dignity? She sighed as her beautiful hat, torn, dusty and misshapen, skipped and bumped its way across the infield far below.

"It didn't suit you anyway," Jack murmured as he reclaimed his seat. "You look better in a motorcycle helmet."

"I'll let the milliners know they're missing out on a trend," she said wryly, not about to let on that his words made her heart skip a beat.

"I predict we have the winners," her father announced as he and Heath returned, tickets in hand.

Heath smiled as he handed her a ticket. "I picked horse number six for you, sweetheart, because the silks are red, and I know it's your favorite color."

Next to her, Jack snorted softly.

Alex squirmed. "Thanks." She shot an irritated glance toward Jack. "Which horse did you bet on?"

His mouth twitched at the corner. "Let's just say that red isn't my favorite color." When Heath and her father sat in the front seats, he added under his breath, "I prefer flesh tones."

She tried not to react, but the man was so outrageous, she couldn't help shaking her head in exasperation.

"I think I see the beginning of a smile," he whispered.

"You're mistaken," she whispered back, determined to keep her mirth under wraps. Jack simply mustn't know how much his nearness affected her.

The tote board ticked down to five minutes until the first race, and the mounted entries were led onto the track by calmer lead horses with their own riders. The crowd hummed louder in anticipation as the horses performed their customary walk down the homestretch of the track, then turned and walked back to the starting line. The jockeys lifted their crops toward the grandstands, churning the spectators into a higher froth.

"Alex," Heath shouted over the din. "Is that *your* hat?" He pointed, his eyebrows high, toward the swollen infield, where the weary hat was still being bandied about.

"Yes," she replied dully, refusing to look at Jack. "It...got away from me."

The starting gate was pulled across the track by a small tractor, and the nail-biting task of loading the horses into the gate was begun. Alex had seen more than one horse and rider injured during this most dangerous part of the race. As was customary, the second the last horse was safely inside, the front gates slammed open, and the horses shot forward.

Alex gave in to the tangible excitement, impossible to ignore as the horses stretched forward until their bodies were almost horizontal. The crowd in the grandstand jumped to their feet in waves. The noise was thunderous as everyone shouted for their chosen mount and the nimble-tongued announcer belted the names of the front runners at every turn. Less than a minute later, the race was over. Horses number two, one and seven came in to win, place and show, and a quick glance at the program revealed the odds on at least two of the entries had been long. Much to her dismay, the number six horse carrying the red-silked jockey not only crossed the finish line last, but way, way behind with a lazy, playful trot that had the audience laughing.

Alex ripped her ticket in half to the tune of Jack's chuckle.

"I only had the show horse," her father said, turning around.

"Nothing for me," Heath said.

Everyone looked to Jack, who seemed remarkably calm.

"Well?" Alex prompted.

His shrug was casual. "I hit the exacta."

Alex glanced at the tote board just as the payout for the exacta—choosing the win and place horses—flashed on the screen. A two dollar bet returned three hundred and fifty dollars, and she suspected that Jack's bet had been more than two dollars.

Her father whooped and Heath pursed his mouth. Alex simply smiled and murmured, "At least you can afford to buy me a new hat."

He didn't answer, simply relaxed in his chair to study the day's racing form, punctuated, she noted, with mysterious notes in the margins, and dotted with curious circles and boxes in various colors.

"Some kind of foolproof system of yours?" she asked, squinting under the glare of the sun.

He handed her his sunglasses, and feeling stubbornly deserving, she took them. "My system isn't quite as scientific as picking the horse based on the jockey's silks," he said, one side of his mouth drawn back.

Scientific or not, his system seemed to work because by

the end of the third race, he'd racked up more winning tickets. Her father had hit a couple of payoffs himself, but she
and Heath had nothing to show for their hit-and-miss
guessing.

"What do you have in the fourth race?" she asked, waving off Heath's offer to place her bet.

"This one's tough," Jack admitted, shaking his head. "The
favorites are so strong, they're bound to win and place, but
they'll only pay out a pittance."

"So?" She leaned over, watching his finger move over the
form as he pointed out subtleties in bloodline, jockeys and
race length. He had nice hands, she observed, her mouth going strangely dry. Large and square-palmed, long, blunt-
tipped fingers, good for catching footballs, she supposed.
With a flash of revelation, she realized how Tremont's new
fine jewelry department could be showcased in the commercials in a way that would appeal to women—she could
put a wedding ring on him. But as quickly as the idea occurred to her, she tabled it, struck by the feeling that a wedding ring on Jack Stillman's finger seemed so unnatural that
it might come across to the audience as being unbelievable.

"What's wrong?" he asked, scrutinizing his hands.

She shook her head, embarrassed. "Um, nothing. I was
just thinking that you must miss playing football."

"Why would you say that?"

Alex shrugged. "It's your identity, isn't it? Jack the Attack?"

Jack nodded, then stood abruptly and mumbled that he
needed to place another bet. Perplexed, she turned to watch
him climb up the concrete steps of the grandstand, noticing
hers wasn't the only pair of feminine eyes following him.
And her chest filled with unreasonable satisfaction that he
was with her today.

Well, not really with *her*, since he'd come as her father's
guest.

A cell phone rang, causing Alex, Heath and her father all to reach for their personal devices.

"It's mine," Heath said, flipping up his phone's antenna and pressing his hand against his opposite ear.

Alex took the opportunity to tell her father about Jack's "plant" with the local sports reporter. "I don't like it, Dad. I thought we agreed he would prove himself first—two weeks, one of which is almost gone, I might add."

"We did."

"Yet he's acting as if he's already a permanent fixture at Tremont's. He didn't even run that little stunt by me first!"

"But you know any publicity is good publicity as long as they spell the name of the store correctly."

"Dad, he's a loose cannon."

"Which means," her father said mildly, "that it's up to you to keep tabs on him."

"But—"

"Honey, like I said before, Jack Stillman is a rebel, and I think he's just what we need around Tremont's to shake everything up a bit. In fact—" he tilted his head and gave her a gently curious look "—if I didn't know better, I'd say Jack had *you* shaken up."

Alex swallowed hard, telling herself not to overreact, yet stunned since her father had never before broached the subject of her personal life. "But you *do* know better," she corrected in a calm tone that belied her panic. Was her attraction to Jack so transparent that even her *father* could tell? She searched his blue eyes, so like her own, looking for comfort, trying to relay her confusion over the men in her life.

Al wet his lips and looked as if he might say something, then was interrupted by Heath flipping his phone closed.

"I hate to do this to you, Alex," Heath said, "but I'm needed at the office."

"What?"

"I'm sorry, sweetheart, but I didn't give my secretary

enough notice to clear my afternoon calendar, and one of my appointments was already on a plane to Lexington when she called to reschedule."

She stood and sighed. "Well, if it can't be helped."

"There's no reason for you to leave," Heath said quickly. "I'm sure your father will be glad to take you home."

Alex looked to her father, who nodded confirmation.

"Okay," she relented, thinking that the day hadn't turned out anything like she'd planned. Still, she could have fun with her father and perhaps start to chip away at the wall erected between them by neglect and indifference. They both were to blame, she realized, studying her father's noble profile—she hadn't exactly extended herself since Gloria had come onto the scene. She vowed to make more of an effort to draw her father closer to her. And when she was a vice president, they'd be working closer together, too.

Heath distracted her from her musings with a quick kiss, and her father left to place a bet on the next race. Alex sat down, feeling restless and warm with the sun bearing down. Since her hat was no longer making the rounds, she imagined it dying a slow, painful death under the feet of tipsy spectators. Her ire rose just thinking about it.

"Shade, milady?"

She looked up to see Jack twirling, of all things, a cream-colored ruffled parasol.

His smile highlighted the cleft in his chin. "I'd hate to be responsible for freckles on that upturned nose of yours."

Despite his backhanded compliment, the picture he presented was simply too incongruous to keep a straight face. "Feeling guilty, are you?"

"Feeling generous," he corrected with a grin as he stepped into the box and slid the frilly umbrella into the hole behind their seats provided for the boxholders who wished to buy the pricey souvenirs. "Since I cashed in on the last race, and since it's down to just the two of us—" Jack stopped when she placed her hand on his arm—not an unwelcome gesture, just surprising.

"What do you mean 'down to just the two of us'?"

Jack pointed over his shoulder with his thumb. "I saw Al upstairs. He said he and Reddinger had to leave, and asked if I would see you home." He watched the emotions play over her face with a sinking realization. "You didn't know?"

She shook her head. "Don't worry, I'll call Heath to come back and pick me up when his meeting is over."

And he'd actually thought she'd agreed to—perhaps even wanted to—spend the rest of the afternoon with him, hence the ridiculous umbrella. "Suit yourself," he said with a mild shrug, not about to admit his acute disappointment, and not sure if he understood his own reaction. Regardless, considering how close he'd come to kissing the woman—and more—the last time he'd taken her home, her alternate plan seemed wise. His promise to Derek ran through his head as if on continuous play. Determined to get his mind off the leggy beauty sitting next to him, he turned his attention to the leggy beauties on the racetrack.

Except his task proved to be harder than he expected, mostly because Alex showed more curiosity in his picks and the reasons behind them. Despite his resolve, he liked having answers to questions she asked—for once. As her interest grew, she placed a couple of bets based on his recommendations, and when their long shot horse came in to place in the next race, she grabbed his arm and jumped up and down. Impulsively, Jack whirled her around and lowered a quick kiss on the cheek. Her eyes widened, but before she could chastise him, he grabbed her hand and pulled her up the steps to collect her payout. Jack blamed his pounding heart on the quick ascent. Derek was right, he conceded—he knew the woman was dangerous, yet he couldn't seem to help himself.

For her part, Alex quietly cashed in her winning ticket, then excused herself to the ladies' room. When she rejoined him at their seats a few minutes later, warning bells sounded in his head because she handed him a beer, and held one of her own. Plus, to his consternation, she'd shed her panty hose somewhere along the way, which gave him even more bare skin to endure. Jack took a long sip of the beer, then held the cool cup to his cheek. Best to steer the conversation back to business as soon as possible.

"I heard you're in the running for a vice presidency."

"Who told you that?"

"Your secretary."

"I should have guessed. The woman's in love with you, you know." She rolled her eyes.

Jack laughed. "So is it true?"

"About the vice presidency? Yes, I'm in the running, along with a few colleagues and a couple of external candidates."

"Who will make the decision?"

"The final call is the board of directors', although they'll probably take the recommendation of the members of senior management and my father."

"Sounds like you're a shoe in," he said carefully. She shook her head and he wondered if he knew how lovely she was—cheeks flushed, the wind picking up the ends of her hair. Her profile was classically tilted, a masterpiece that made his fingers itch for a stick of waxy pastels, or a vine of drawing charcoal to get the lines down on paper. He hadn't drawn anything for his own pleasure in years.

"I won't get favorable treatment simply because of my last name," she said. "In fact, my father is so concerned about nepotism, sometimes I think he errs in the other direction." She looked over at him with a rueful smile. "Sorry, you probably think that sounds like sour grapes."

"No." He wasn't inclined to criticize the one insightful

tidbit she'd offered him into her personal and professional life.

"I'm actually very grateful for having the chance to learn from my father. He's a brilliant retailer who somehow seems to stay ahead of the trends even though he hasn't bought a new suit in ten years."

Jack smiled. "A great observer of the human condition."

She nodded, then took a small sip of her beer. "Although I can't say I always agree with him."

He lifted his cup for a drink. "Like his decision to hire me, for instance?"

She sighed. "Jack, you and I both know that *my* father hired you because of a spontaneous promise he made to *your* father, and because of your notoriety. Can you see why I'm a little skeptical? I've seen your office, remember. I know how limited your resources are. If I weren't concerned, I wouldn't be fulfilling my responsibility to the company."

Jack felt a stab of remorse for not stopping to consider the awkward position Alex must be in—follow her father, or follow her conscience. For the first time in his life, he wished he was successful by conventional standards, successful enough to give Alex confidence in his ability. Funny, but she was the only person—definitely the only woman—who hadn't taken him at face value. He was going to have to earn her trust, and respect. The fact that he was the cause of the little crease in her brow caused his gut to clench. "Alex," he said quietly, "I realize you have no reason to believe me, but I won't let you down."

She studied him for a few seconds, then tilted her head, a smile playing on her full lips. "I'm not certain, but I think I like this side of you."

Jack's pulse kicked up. "What side is that?"

"The almost-serious, professional side."

Did a more beautiful pair of eyes exist in the world? He

gestured toward her, head to toe. "I think I like this side of you."

Her thin, arched eyebrows rose. "What side is that?"

He grinned. "The beer-drinking, bare-legged gambler."

She blushed, then looked back to the track. "Which proves," she said, her voice featherlight, but deadly serious, "that anyone can playact for a few hours, but at the end of the day, we are who we are."

The bell announcing the start of the next race sounded, and her attention was diverted to the running of the maiden race that featured the granddaughter of Spectacular Wish. She leapt to her feet, cheering their underachiever on to victory. Jack was so distracted watching her and reveling in the elated hug she gave him afterward, he almost forgot to be glad for the chunk of change he'd just won. If he didn't know better, he'd have sworn that a subtle shift in their relationship had occurred during their abbreviated conversation.

Whatever the cause, Alex did seem more relaxed as the last couple of races were run. "It's much better when you're winning," she said, her eyes as bright as a child's as he removed the parasol in begrudged preparation to leave. The crowd, mostly losers for the day, had begun to dissipate much earlier in order to avoid the rush of exiting traffic. Suddenly her mouthed rounded to an O. "I forgot to call Heath!"

Jack closed his fingers around her wrist as she delved into her purse, presumably for her cellular phone. "I'll drive you—I need to pick up my jacket anyway." He told himself it was a good reason to put himself in an otherwise risky situation of being alone with Alex at her place. She stared down at his hand, and he reluctantly released her.

But she didn't retrieve her phone.

Instead, she struck out ahead of him, parasol twirling

over her shoulder, and tossed back, "You're pretty confident for a man who destroyed my new hat."

Thoughts of hurrying to catch up with her were dismissed when he caught sight of her curvy sway. This was one woman he wouldn't mind walking a few steps behind for the rest of his—er, for a while. "Like I said, it didn't suit you."

"I know," she said, her voice sarcastic. "I look much better in a motorcycle helmet, my eyes squeezed shut, and holding on for dear life."

"Well," he drawled, loving the way the soft, long skirt of her dress floated up as she walked, revealing the backs of her knees and the curve of her calves. "I'm partial to that 'holding on for dear life' part." He nearly plowed into the back of her when she stopped abruptly to give him a pointed look.

"Okay," Jack pulled a snowy handkerchief from his back pocket and waved it in surrender. "I'll behave."

She shook her head, but he'd seen her look much more angry. Unbelievably buoyed, Jack steered her in the direction of his bike, parked on a knoll inaccessible by most vehicles. He withdrew his extra helmet and helped her strap it on snugly, tucking strands of dark lush hair beneath the face edge. Her skin was velvety smooth beneath his knuckles.

"You must have lots of passengers if you carry an extra helmet," she remarked.

He shrugged, poking at a stubborn strand next to her eye. "I suppose."

"Any passengers who are more, um, *regular* than others?"

Jack stopped his ministrations, but she was studying her fingernails. Was she asking what he thought she was asking? "Just one," he said, giving her chin strap a final tug. "In fact, I bought the helmet for her."

"Oh."

Jack pulled on his own helmet, threw his leg over the seat,

then lifted the kickstand with an upward jerk and forward roll. He reached back to flip down the footpegs, then braced for her to climb on.

Alex frowned down at her dress. "This is going to be awkward."

He grinned. "I promise not to look." With fingers crossed on the handlebar grips, he turned his gaze forward—to take in the entire show in the side mirror. Between the unwieldy lowered parasol she held under her arm, the big purse, and her voluminous skirt, she was quite the performer. And her pale-colored panties, it seemed, were trimmed with scalloped lace. He stifled a groan as she settled in behind him, sitting as stiffly as one of her store mannequins.

He started the engine, then said, "Relax." Rolling his shoulders, he reveled in the feeling of her breasts pressed against him.

She did relax, a millimeter or two, as he maneuvered through the traffic at a leisurely pace. When they came to a stop in a line of exiting traffic, Alex lifted her head and looked around.

"Are you comfortable?" he asked.

She nodded, and after a few minutes, she cleared her throat. "This, um, regular passenger of yours—she must be very important if she warrants her own helmet."

"She is," Jack assured her. "But then Mom has always been pretty close to my heart." He winked at her in the side mirror, boosted by her unexpected smile. On impulse, he covered her hand curled around his waist with his own, instantly struck by the softness of her skin and his desire to entwine their fingers. "Hold on for dear life," he warned in his most ominous voice, then begrudgingly released her hand and accelerated, cutting out of the traffic and threading the bike toward Versailles Road.

He took the long way to Alex's downtown apartment, telling himself in the beginning he was avoiding the worst of the traffic, but finally admitting to himself that he was prolonging their ride for his own selfish purposes, relishing the feel of her slender body melded to his. When his round-about route came to an end in her parking lot, he was already looking forward to Monday—not because he would be filming the commercials, but because he would be seeing Alex again.

The knowledge spooked him so much, he could barely help her undo her helmet. "Before long, you'll be a pro," he teased, then realized he was implying that she would be riding with him again...and often.

She blinked those beautiful blue eyes, while running her fingers through her loose hair. "Is this motorcycle your only transportation?"

"Yep. If the weather is bad, I usually borrow my brother's car." He smiled down at her, caught up in her beauty shining in the light of early dusk. Yet his reference to his brother reminded him of his promise. "I'll just walk you up, grab my jacket, and be on my way."

He followed her through the stairwell and up three flights to her apartment, this time keeping his gaze squarely on the back of her head. When Alex unlocked her door and walked inside, he hung back, thinking the hallway was the safest spot in the vicinity. Alex obliged by returning quickly with his jacket dangling from her long-fingered hand.

"Thanks," he said, taking the jacket, but suddenly unable to move. "I guess I'll see you Monday at the studio."

She nodded.

Ordering his feet to retreat, Jack said, "Have a nice evening."

"Jack."

"Yeah?"

"Thanks for...a fun day."

"See," he said, reaching forward to brush that same stubborn strand of silky dark hair from her flushed cheek. "You *can* have fun if you let yourself." He'd been trying to get Alex to loosen up, but now he realized his resistance was far more secure when fending off her barbed tongue, rather than wondering how it tasted.

Before he had time to change his mind, he cupped his hand around the back of her neck and lowered his mouth to hers for a quick kiss that turned exploratory as soon as his mouth met hers. A day's worth of teasing and restraint poured into the kiss. Knowing it might well be his only one, Jack foraged her mouth thoroughly, savoring the sweetness of her flavor. His body, already keen for her, vaulted to painful awareness of her proximity. When she moaned into his mouth, he pulled her against him, divulging how much she excited him.

When a noise sounded behind him in the hall, Jack lifted his head to see remorse flash in Alex's eyes as her gaze darted to the person walking toward them, humming.

"Oh!" A tall woman with spiky white hair stopped short, her eyes round as she eyed them both. "Pardon me, I...I...never mind." She turned on her platform heels and disappeared around the corner at a pace somewhere between a jog and a sprint.

He looked back to Alex, his eyebrows high, his lips stinging, his erection straining.

"My n-neighbor," she explained, pulling back and touching her mouth absently. Her chest rose and fell quickly and a frown marred her forehead. "Jack, about what just happened—"

At her agonized tone, he held up his hand and plastered a glib smile on his face. "A little friendly curiosity—now satisfied."

A myriad of emotions played over her face, then she appeared immensely relieved. "Right. Well...thanks again for the ride home. Good night."

Wringing his jacket, he stared at her closed door for several seconds, wondering what might have ensued without the appearance of Alex's neighbor. Nothing wise, he was certain. As he retraced his steps to his bike, Alex's earlier words came back to him.

Anyone can playact for a few hours, but at the end of the day, we are who we are. Amen to that, Jack thought, grateful for the interruption. And he couldn't imagine two people at farther ends of the spectrum than he and Alexandria Tremont: She was a purebred, he was a mongrel. She was the princess, he was the pea.

He scratched his temple as he straddled the seat. Funny, but he couldn't remember ever wanting to be anything other than what he was. Until now.

Jack glanced up at the white and yellow lights emanating from Alex's windows, spilling over the black wrought iron rail of her balcony. With the onset of darkness, the warm lights glowed like a beacon. What the devil was this woman doing to him?

12

STILL SHAKEN from the intensity of Jack's kiss, Alex disrobed in a daze, then stepped under a warm shower, figuring she had about ten minutes before Lana returned demanding details, although her neighbor would be mightily disappointed since Alex herself wasn't even sure what had happened. She leaned her head back and allowed the warm water to run over her body—nice, but a poor substitute for a man's hands.

Jack's hands, she realized with dismay, wondering if her startling attraction to him had something to do with her somewhat stale relationship with Heath. Using a bar of raspberry scented soap, she lathered her body with a rich layer of suds, luxuriating in the aroma.

The kiss had simply...happened. What had he said? *A little friendly curiosity—now satisfied.* She frowned as she rinsed her hair. It certainly hadn't taken him long to decide she wasn't worth the trouble.

She emerged from the soothing spray reluctantly, and dressed slowly in cotton leggings and an oversized T-shirt that she knotted at her waist.

After all, a girl had feelings.

Opting to let her hair dry naturally, she crossed to the kitchen and opened the refrigerator door on the off chance that a veggie pizza from Malone's had materialized in her absence. It hadn't.

Obviously she wasn't as hot as the women he was used to...having.

Morose, she stuck her finger into the carton of fudge icing for an unhealthy gob of the stuff, and sucked it off as she wandered around the apartment feeling restless and prickly. She turned on the television and flicked through the channels before switching it off again. She considered calling Heath, but for some reason she resisted, stubbornly clinging to the electrical awareness she'd experienced when Jack kissed her. Wise or not, the desire still swimming in her stomach felt good. Exhilarating. Had Heath's kisses ever made her feel so disoriented and foolhardy? Surely she would have remembered this, this, this *bizarre* jittery sensation.

Alex dropped into her favorite chair and leaned her head back with a sigh, hugging a pillow to her chest. So she lusted for the man—so schlep her into the same category as every other woman who crossed his wayward path. With a wry smile she acknowledged that as much as she liked to think she pursued lofty, esoteric goals, she wasn't above base passion.

What a blow to realize that sex, not commerce, made the world go around.

But what a relief to know that she was capable of the kind of desire that Lana espoused.

Right on cue, the rapid knock on her door announced the arrival of her friend. Anxious to unload her new revelation, despite the ribbing she knew she was due, Alex abandoned the pillow, padded to the door, then swung it open.

But her pulse spiked when Jack's broad shadow fell across her doorway, swallowing her. He stood, hands at his sides, legs wide, head slightly bowed, his face obscured in the darkness. Her throat tightened, squeezing off her ability to talk as reasons for him returning raced through her mind. He was having engine trouble. He wanted to discuss Monday's shoot. He wanted to grab a bite to eat somewhere. He needed directions.

"I came back to finish what we started."

Or he'd come back to finish what they'd started. She swallowed as the raw longing in his voice cut through her. It was crazy, the way her body responded to the magnetism emanating from him. Crazy and wonderfully overwhelming, and worthy of exploration. Before she could process a rational thought, Alex stepped forward, looped her arms around his neck, and pulled his mouth down to hers. His gladdened groan sent a wake-up call to every nerve in her body, and his arms moved fluidly to encircle her waist. His lips were hungry, hard, urgent. His body was taut for her, and the knowledge sent moisture to the juncture of her thighs.

Reaching lower to cup her bottom, he lifted her off her feet and carried her inside. He kicked the door closed behind them. She lost track of time and their direction, but was gratified sometime later to feel the softness of her bed at her back. Her thighs opened to accommodate him as he stretched atop her. He pressed her deep into the covers, his body alive with movement—his mouth devouring hers, his hands beneath her, pulling her hips against his hardness.

His blatant desire for her fueled the destruction of her own inhibitions. Alex summoned the energy to push at the leather jacket around his shoulders, forcing him to shift and shed the garment. His gaze locked with hers, his eyes heavy-lidded and glazed, his open lips transferring air in and out of his lungs with heavy gasps. She moved in a liquid haze, carried along by a tide of passion. With one quick jerk, the snaps on the front of his denim shirt were freed, laying his chest bare to her seeking fingers. In another second, the shirt was gone. She scarcely had time to register the corded beauty of his upper body before he tugged the knot of her shirt loose and shimmied the thin material over her head to bare her to the waist as well.

After a glance of appreciation that warmed her, he fell

upon her, his palms closing around her breasts, coning the tips for his seeking mouth. Alex cried aloud when he suckled her, reveling in the brush of his chest hair against her skin. He drew her flesh deep into his hot mouth, his moan vibrating against her sensitive nipple. Nearly blind with wanting him, Alex threaded her fingers through his hair and urged him to draw harder. At her insistence, his tending escalated from gentle laving to little bites that left her twitching. Slowly, he kissed a trail to her waistband, then pushed himself to his feet, rolling her thin pants down her legs as he stood.

Jack was so worked up at the thought of making love to Alex that he nearly came at the sight of her nudity, a jolt to his already electrified system. She was breathtaking—long-limbed and toned, with high, jutting breasts, and a slender waist that gave way to a generous swell of hip and taut thighs. Gritting his teeth for control, he leaned forward, grasped her by the waist, and pulled her to the edge of the bed, loving the contrast of her dark hair splayed against the white comforter, loving more that the tall bed was just the right height for him to make love to her in a most enjoyable position.

With little urging, she opened her knees, revealing the glistening pink petals of her womanhood, sending her musky scent to torment him further. With rapidly vanishing restraint, he stood between her knees, probing her with careful fingers, readying her for his body until her moans and undulations became too much to endure. Feeling like a schoolboy in his haste, Jack fumbled with the front of his pants. It was as if his body had never done this before, a reaction that triggered a small alarm in the recesses of his blood-deprived brain. At last he freed his raging erection, which answered her mewling call with a few drops of oozing lubrication. Never before had he been tempted to skip a condom, which in and of itself sobered him enough to slow down for a heartbeat. Fishing in his back pocket for his wallet, he prayed he'd replaced the last one he'd used, because only a word of refusal from Alex could stop him now, protection or no.

His knees practically buckled with relief when he found one, and he set a record rolling it on. A split second of guilt barbed through him for not at least removing his jeans, but Alex already had him so close to the brink, he didn't want to risk taking the time. And if truth be known, he wanted her so badly, he couldn't bear the thought of another delay. Trembling with anticipation, he pulled her knees to his waist and pushed the tip of his erection against her wetness. Her leg muscles tensed and a moan tore from her lips as he thrust inside her unbelievably tight channel, setting his jaw for maximum restraint against the torrent of fire that consumed him.

He moved cautiously, filling her and retreating with climbing desire. Jack was struck by the erotic sight of her, arms wide, hands fisted in the white comforter, back arched, breasts high, mouth moving with alternate coos and gasps. Her vocal responses bolstered his confidence that he was stimulating her in the way she wanted, and carried his own climax close to the surface. He coaxed her to his plane, drawing her legs up to rest against his shoulders, kissing her ankles as he thrust deeper and deeper and murmuring how incredible she felt wrapped around him. Escalation of the noises emerging from her throat alerted him that she was nearing climax, driving him to thrust harder and faster while tensing to contain his own release.

From her body's state of disarray, Alex sensed the approaching orgasm would surpass her previous experiences, but she wasn't prepared for the mind-numbing, muscle-stealing explosion of euphoria that broke over her body in waves. Shameless in her abandon, she cried out his name, bucking against the steel rod of his flesh imbedded in her.

She had just started to descend to Earth when Jack's body went rigid and he growled his release against her leg. Alex reveled in the light pressure of his teeth, the hot blasts of his ragged breath on her skin.

He was magnificent in the dim lighting, the toned planes of his stomach contracting and relaxing in quick spasms. She was fascinated by the juncture of their bodies, which seemed almost surreal. His jeans rode just low enough on his lean hips to allow his body access to hers, a sharp contrast to her complete nakedness. As cool air hit her body, Alex began to feel exposed, and whispers of remorse nudged at her. She moved to disengage their bodies, eliciting a clutching groan from Jack. He held her to him while controlling his careful withdrawal, a satisfied smile on his handsome face.

Alex eased back onto the pillows at the head of her bed, her body singing with completion, humming with unimagined indulgence. She clung to the sensation of their mutual pleasure, postponing the inevitable regret.

Jack, on the other hand, seemed undaunted by their indiscretion. He pulled away the sheet when she attempted to cover herself, and kissed her breasts leisurely. "You are so incredibly beautiful," he whispered against her skin, evoking another wave of desire through her body. Within the space of a heartbeat, he drew her back into the tantalizing languor of his embrace, nuzzling her neck, kissing her thoroughly before rolling over to lie next to her. His sigh fanned her temple.

"I didn't mean for this to happen," he said, "but I'd be lying if I said I hadn't thought about it since the first time we met."

Alex closed her eyes, berating herself. She'd imagined a budding emotional connection between them today, when they'd really only shared a few laughs, a few drinks, and a few looks. He'd wanted to sleep with her from the beginning, so he'd behaved accordingly. Yes, they'd developed a rapport. Yes, they'd had fun. Yes, they were physically compatible. But she'd been so desperate for that elusive...soul mate...that she'd conjured up feelings between them that simply didn't exist. Darn Lana and all her talk about passion.

"Are you sleeping?" he whispered.

"No," she managed to say. "Just thinking."

"Hey, don't get too deep on me," he teased. "Is your bathroom close by?"

A stone of comprehension fell to the bottom of her stomach. Speechless, she gestured toward the door, her vision blurred with tears as she watched him cross to the bathroom, his pants still undone.

When the door closed, she covered her face with her hands. What had she done? Spread her legs for Jack Stillman, a man she neither liked nor respected, and someone she'd have to work with for at least the next several days. She moved jerkily from the bed to yank on her discarded clothing, biting back a sob when her ring caught on her T-shirt. With a shaky hand, she hung Jack's shirt from a bedpost, then hastily smoothed the telltale wrinkles from the white comforter.

If only the episode could be so easily erased from her mind, she acknowledged with a trembling sigh. She'd never been loose with her body, had never handed over the precious commodity of herself without a level of emotional commitment from her partner. So why now, why Jack Stillman? Sure, he was handsome, but Lexington had its share of nice-looking men.

Alex sank her teeth into her lower lip. *Heath.* Oh, no, what had she done?

When the bathroom door opened, she nearly jumped out of her skin. Jack emerged wearing a smile, the fly of his jeans still zipped, but unbuttoned. Sex appeal rolled off the man's naked torso, necessitating the need to turn her back. At the sound of his approaching footsteps, she realized that he still wore his riding boots, just another reminder that their encounter had been quick and dirty.

"I'm hungry," he murmured into her ear from behind, his arms snaking around her middle.

"I'm not," she said distinctly, unlocking his hands and walking out of his embrace.

"What's this?"

She inhaled deeply, then turned to face him, arms folded over her breasts, which still tingled from his touch. "What's what?"

He frowned, hands on lean hips. "This attitude."

Alex swallowed, terrified that he looked so good to her, even after their hurried sex. The episode was obviously nothing unusual for him—he probably knocked on doors and wound up in strange beds all the time. A man like Jack would never understand what a monumental mistake their few minutes together represented to her. Keeping her voice level, she said, "You need to fasten your pants and leave, Jack."

One eyebrow arrowed up. "That's it? Fasten my pants and leave?" His voice was low, but tinged with anger.

His response fueled her defenses, causing her to lash out. "So sorry if most of your conquests provide more than one round."

His mouth tightened, but otherwise, he didn't move.

The longer the silence stretched between them, the more unsure Alex was of her ability to resist him again. The man had a way of mastering a room and the people in it. She had thought herself immune to his uncanny charisma, but had never been so wrong. Unable to break eye contact with him, Alex watched him walk toward her, seemingly in slow motion. With his every step her resolve crumbled, and with a sinking dread, she realized where they were once again headed.

A knock on her door halted his progress, and she sighed with relief. Lana to the rescue. Alex turned to the door and called, "Lana, I'm a little busy right now."

"Alex," Heath said, and the sound of his voice sent terror to her heart.

She turned wide eyes toward Jack, who seemed almost...amused? Gesturing wildly, she hissed, "You have to get out of here!"

"Why?" he whispered. "I locked the door—just don't let him in."

"He has a key," she whispered back, her heart thudding in her ears. Heath did not deserve to find another man in her apartment. Louder, she called, "Give me a minute and I'll be right there." Desperate, she ran to retrieve Jack's shirt. "You have to hide!"

He caught his shirt and shrugged into it, then fastened his jeans. "I will *not* hide just because you can't admit the truth to your boyfriend."

Alex stopped, facing him. "And what truth would that be?"

"That he obviously doesn't satisfy you."

Her face flamed in the face of her wantonness. "I love Heath," she said calmly.

"Oh, you *love* him? Well, your loyalty is staggering."

His sarcasm stung her like a slap. She imagined all kinds of scenes if Heath and Jack squared off in her apartment, Jack gloating, Heath the cuckold. She hated herself, and she hated Jack Stillman. "If you have a decent bone in your body, you won't do this," Alex managed to say.

"I'll just use my key," Heath announced, and she closed her eyes, tensing for a confrontation. She opened her eyes at the sound of a door sliding open, just in time to see the blue of Jack's shirt disappearing over the railing of her balcony.

The sheer curtains billowed inside the apartment, dancing on the breeze. Before she could react, Heath opened the door, and she wheeled to give him a smile she snatched from thin air.

He gave her a quick embrace, but all Alex could think was that the aroma of another man's lovemaking lingered on her body. "Enjoying the balcony?" Heath asked, nodding toward the open door.

"Um, no, not exactly," Alex said, slipping out of his arms and crossing to the open door. "The insects are so bad, you know." She slid the door closed, just in time to muffle the low rumble of a motorcycle starting. At least the cad hadn't broken his neck, she thought with a tiny rush of relief.

"Your bug zapper isn't working?" Heath asked behind her.

"Not on this particular pest," she murmured to the glass door, watching the single taillight disappear at a breathtaking speed.

13

"OKAY, ALEX, I have a fifteen minute break, so you'd better talk fast." Lana set a mug of steaming coffee in front of Alex and plopped down in the opposite café chair.

"Who says I have something to talk *about*?" Alex was already reconsidering her impulse to stop by to see her friend before putting in a few hours at the office on a Saturday morning.

Lana looked toward the ceiling. "I'm assuming this impromptu visit has something to do with the grinding fullbody kiss you shared with Jack the Attack last night, followed by his subsequent return, then Heath's appearance, and my next door neighbor's shrieking phone call that some man was scaling down the fire escape ladder from your apartment."

Stunned, Alex swallowed a huge mouthful of coffee. "I didn't realize I was under surveillance."

"Our cable was finally cut off, and the traffic in and out of your apartment was more interesting than watching static."

"Gee, thanks."

"Just be glad I was able to talk Mrs. Standish out of calling the police," Lana said. "Holy hickey—is that a *bite* mark on your leg?"

Choking on the coffee she sucked down her windpipe, Alex's gaze flew to the area between her ankle and calf, the pink imprint of Jack's perfect teeth clearly visible on her bare leg below the hem on her long floral skirt. She hadn't noticed it this morning, but then again, she wasn't accustomed to checking her body for telltale love bites, either. Alex quickly crossed her legs at the knee, tucking the offensive mark out of sight. "I, um...I, um..."

"You're blushing again," her friend said with a whoop. "So, was he as fantastic a lover as he was rumored to be in college?"

Alex massaged her temples, wondering if she should unload her grievous mistake on her friend or let it fester inside her until she ruptured from guilt. Finally, she sighed and nodded morosely.

Lana squealed. "I knew it! The best you've ever had?"

Her dignity long gone, she winced and nodded again.

Another squeal. "How *romantic*—your lover sneaking down the fire escape as your fiancé walks through the front door!"

"Lana, it wasn't romantic, it was lunacy. It was deceitful. Heath is a decent man who deserves better." She stared into the depths of her coffee, wishing she'd been thinking as clearly last night as she was this morning.

Her friend was studying her with those disconcerting violet eyes. "Oh, my God. You're falling for Jack Stillman, aren't you?"

Alex's eyes bulged from her aching head. "You can't be serious. I don't even *like* Jack Stillman."

"Disdain keeps a relationship interesting. Look at my folks."

"Lana, for heaven's sake, there's no 'relationship' here. The man is a playboy, heavy emphasis on the 'boy.'"

"He looked full-grown from my vantage point."

She scoffed. "He probably went home and carved a notch in the post of his waterbed."

Lana lifted a pale eyebrow. "Just one notch?"

Alex rolled her eyes. "Yeeeeees."

"Did you tell Heath?"

"No."

"Good—take this one to your grave."

"Considering I almost had a stroke last night when Heath showed up, I nearly *did* take it to my grave. He only stayed long enough to have a drink, but I was an absolute nervous wreck by the time he left." She exhaled noisily. "I should have told him last night. Instead I was awake all night, wallowing in guilt."

"Alex, you're too uptight. You and Heath aren't married yet, you know."

"But we're supposed to be setting a date soon!"

"Life is all about timing, girlfriend."

Alex frowned, reluctant to unleash that particular line of thinking.

Lana tilted her head. "Hmm—loose hair, pink cheeks, bright eyes. If you ask me, depravity suits you."

"You know, if you don't buy this coffee shop, you really should consider counseling."

"Me, be a counselor?"

"No, I meant you should *see* a counselor."

"Oh, very funny. You know, a black widow spider also turns hostile after good sex."

Alex stuck her tongue out at her friend.

"So, when will you see him again?"

"Who?"

"Jack!"

Alex sighed, certain there was no more miserable, sinful person walking the streets. "Monday. I'm supervising a combination commercial and photo shoot. I don't have the slightest idea what I'll say when I see him."

"I wouldn't worry about it. Men tend not to obsess over illicit sex. They save their energy for bigger things like professional wrestling...and eating foods that end in *o.*"

"Well, I'm sure you're right about one thing," Alex observed wryly. "Jack Stillman hasn't lost a wink of sleep over our little encounter."

JACK YAWNED for the umpteenth time, cursing the insomnia brought on by wondering if Reddinger stayed at Alex's apartment last night. More than the lost sleep, though, he simply hated the feeling of helplessness and frustration, and that he was letting it get to him. After all, he'd only known the woman for a few days. If it didn't bother her to cheat on her boyfriend, why should it bother him?

He banged his fist on his desk. Because, dammit, it had taken all his nerve to go back to her apartment and risk making a fool out of himself. He'd hoped she felt the chemistry between them that had his senses on a tilt, but he couldn't be sure. He couldn't read this woman—she was different than the females he was accustomed to. Cold, hot, smart, gorgeous, engaged, sexy, engaged, passionate. Engaged.

He resented like hell sneaking over her balcony like a blasted criminal while blankety-blank Reddinger marched in the freaking front door like a bloody king. And it stuck in his craw to realize that what had been a fairly relevant experience for him had been little more than a tumble to Alex.

You need to fasten your pants and leave, Jack.

At the memory of her words, he muttered a few more choice words of his own into his thick, cold coffee. He'd never been asked to leave a woman's place before, except by the occasional rankled boyfriend or brother or father. He'd made the mistake of thinking that because their passion had been electric for him, that it had been for Alex, too. Apparently, that wasn't the case.

He should have taken more time with her, he thought, chastising himself. Been more gentle, more—he grimaced— sensitive. But the woman had him so worked up, it was a miracle he'd lasted as long as he did. He'd told himself that he would take his time when they made love again, which would have been before morning if he'd had his way. Alex wasn't the kind of woman a man could sample—he wanted his fill of her, and it irked him like the dickens that she didn't share his sentiments.

Jack stopped and frowned. Sentiments? Bad choice of words.

When another yawn overtook him, he stood to limp around his desk on the ankle he'd sprained when he dropped from the end of the fire escape ladder. He sighed, running his hand down his face. At least the office was blessedly quiet. Tuesday, thankfully, believed in weekends off from her non-paying job. And Stripling the Fed definitely wouldn't be bothering him on a Saturday. So he was determined to finish several drawings today for the Tremont's account and a few other odds and ends—if he could stay awake.

When the phone rang, he was tempted to let it go, then, buoyed by the slim chance that Alex might be trying to reach him, he yanked up the receiver. "Stillman & Sons Agency, Jack speaking."

"Well, I *don't* believe it," his brother Derek said. "You in the office on a Saturday."

Jack winced, not in the mood to hear from his brother— Derek was having all the sex he could withstand with a woman he cared about.

Not that he actually *cared* about Alex, Jack reminded himself.

"Are you there, Jack?"

"Yeah, I'm here." Naturally, he didn't want anything bad to happen to the woman, but that wasn't the same as *caring* about her.

"You don't sound so good, bro. Late night?"

"Not particularly. Just a little tired." Because if getting naked with Alexandria Tremont was foolish, *caring* about her would be just plain stupid.

"How's the Tremont account going?"

"I'm working on it now. Thought I'd put in a few hours,

before going to the football game with old man Tremont this afternoon." Because the poor man who lost himself in those blue eyes of hers was doomed to a life of servitude.

"I'm impressed. In the office on a Saturday and shmoozing the client, too. If I didn't know better, Jack, I'd say you were...working."

"I see marriage has turned you into a comedian," Jack remarked dryly. Although a life of servitude between the thighs of the exquisite Alexandria held a certain amount of appeal.

"So, have you managed to wow the boss's daughter— what's her name?"

"Alexandria. And I wouldn't exactly use the word 'wow' yet." Although, dammit, if he could just convince her to give him another chance between the sheets, he'd rock her world.

"You'll do all right if you can keep your libido under control."

Jack frowned, realizing that, once again, Derek was right. He'd probably blown his only chance to win over Alex by dragging her to bed like a Neanderthal. Once Reddinger and her father found out, they'd kick him off the account for sure. Then he straightened with a revelation.

What if she'd set him up? How convenient that good ol' Reddinger had shown up last night when he did. Maybe she'd concocted the entire scheme to get rid of Jack and secure the other firm she'd wanted to work with all along. He gulped. And as much as Al Tremont liked him, he might draw the line at Jack the Attack diddling his precious daughter. In fact, if Derek wanted to kill him for bedding Ms. Tremont, he might have to stand in line.

"Jack," Derek said. "You *are* keeping your word to not get involved with this woman, aren't you?"

Remorse washed over him that he'd jeopardized the acccount, and worse, that he'd imagined Alexandria *wanted* him. "Derek, we're not involved," he said thickly. Alex had made that much perfectly clear, hadn't she? *You need to fasten your pants and leave, Jack.*

Now that he looked back on the episode, he felt downright used. Like a...a...a piece of meat.

"Well, that's a relief," Derek said. "Promise me you'll be on your best behavior."

"Yeah, I promise." A rather *large* piece of meat, but meat nonetheless.

"Anything else going on I should know about?"

"Um, no, not a thing." Jack leaned down to massage his throbbing ankle. He didn't have the time or energy to launch into the office problems, plus he didn't want to wreck the rest of Derek's honeymoon. "How's Hawaii?"

"Great," Derek said. "What little we've seen of it."

"Bad weather?"

"No, good sex. I figure we can buy a postcard book or something at the airport when we leave."

Jack chuckled. "Janine has really loosened you up, man."

"Yeah, it's amazing how a woman can change you."

When an image of Alex's face flashed in his mind, Jack suddenly sobered. "That's assuming a man needs to be changed."

"Yeah, well, we're not all perfect like you, Jack. Hey, I have to go—Janine just yelled for me."

"And you jump when she calls?"

"Like a randy kangaroo," Derek said cheerfully. "You just wait, man, a woman's going to come along someday and blindside you, too."

Jack frowned and hung up the phone. He didn't begrudge his brother happiness—God knew he deserved it. But he'd become one of those I-found-the-meaning-of-life-and-you-need-it-too-brotha-and-sista married people. No, thanks.

Pure resolve drove him to finish the drawings in record

time, which he tucked into a portfolio. Since he was picking up Al at his office, he'd stop on the way and make color copies to leave on Alex's desk so she'd have them before the photo and commercial shoot on Monday. The drawings were good and maybe they would prevent his ass from being fired, if his suspicions regarding Alex's wiles were confirmed.

Jack sighed, mentally kicking himself with every step through the parking lot. He'd find out soon enough, he supposed.

"SEND THE TRAY OF RINGS to my office as soon as possible, please." Alex hung up the phone and made a check mark on the inventory of items she was gathering for the shoot on Monday. At this rate, she'd need a van to get Jack's wardrobe and props to the studio. She sat at her desk, too restless and distracted by the events of the previous evening to address anything but the most superficial items on her to-do list.

Snatches of their hurried lovemaking flashed through her mind, unbidden. If she closed her eyes, she could still feel his hands on her, could still feel their bodies joined. But when she opened her eyes, all she could feel was the blanket of guilt settling over her head. She wasn't sure what had come over her last night when Jack had returned to her door, but so far she had ruled out common sense, rationality and coherence.

Leaning forward on her elbows, Alex pressed her fingers to her temples and admitted the awful truth. *She had wanted him.* Blame it on being thrown off balance by his sudden appearance at the racetrack, blame it on the disappointment of Heath leaving early, blame it on the proximity to Jack the rest of the afternoon, blame it on the weather, but she had wanted him in the most base way a woman could want a man. Worse, she wanted him again.

At the short rap on her door, Alex turned, relieved at the sight of her father standing in the doorway. They had the whole afternoon together, just the two of them—just the tonic she needed to put Jack Stillman out of her mind. "Are you ready to leave for the gallery?" she asked, reaching for her purse, then hesitated at the sight of his rather casual clothing.

"Alex, dear, I'm sorry. I left you a message at your apartment this morning, but you must have already left. Would you mind if I take a rain check on the gallery showing?"

Disappointment barbed through her, but she managed a shrug. "Has something come up?"

"Actually—hey, Jack!" He waved with animation in the direction of the elevators.

Alex's heart jumped to her throat. "Jack?" she croaked.

"He invited me to the UK football game this afternoon. You don't mind if you and I reschedule, do you, dear?"

She did mind, but one look at his shining face told her where and with whom he'd rather spend the day. Her heart squeezed. "Of course I d-don't mind, Dad." Then she tensed, waiting for the appearance of Jack, wishing she'd had more time to prepare for this face-to-face meeting.

The day was rapidly going in the tank.

Looking well-rested and fit in jeans and a gray UK sweatshirt, Jack stepped into the doorway and shook hands with her father. The men made small talk, ignoring her, but giving her time to gather her wits.

Her heart thumped crazily as she scrutinized the length of him, struck by his incredible good looks, remembering their intimate encounter, the things they'd whispered to each other in the throes of passion. Her temperature climbed and the collar of her blouse suddenly seemed warm against her neck.

"Hello, Alex," he said finally, smiling in her direction.

"Hello, Jack," she responded, just as if they had no carnal knowledge of each other whatsoever.

"I brought a few drawings to leave with you," he said, patting a portfolio he held under his arm.

"You kids can chat," her father said. "I'll wrap up a few things on my desk."

"Ten minutes?" Jack asked him.

Her father winked and clapped Jack on the shoulder. "You got it, son."

Jealousy gripped her stomach at the easy camaraderie between her father and this virtual stranger, something she and her father would never have. When Al retreated and Jack walked into her office, she swallowed hard. On the other hand, if she could *sleep* with this virtual stranger, why shouldn't her father enjoy a mere afternoon of football with him?

"Hi," he said, with the smallest smile.

She matched his expression. "I thought we got past that point already."

"I left my jacket at your place again."

Alex crossed her arms, glad for the comforting barrier of her desk. "Along with your teeth print on my leg."

His eyebrow shot up and for a split second he looked proud of himself, then recovered. "Sorry about that."

"That's okay," she said, anxious to put the lapse behind them. "It won't happen again."

He scratched his temple, and nodded. "I agree."

She blinked. "Good." She wasn't sure what kind of reaction she'd expected, but meek acquiescence wasn't on the list. Which obviously meant that he'd found their tryst less than remarkable. To change the subject, she pointed to the portfolio. "You have some drawings to show me?"

He nodded, walking toward her desk.

"Are you limping?"

"Uh, yeah, I twisted it last night when I was leaving."

Alex bit back a smile as she took the portfolio. "Are you okay?"

He looked a little sheepish. "I'll survive. Listen, I overheard your father when I walked up. I didn't mean to take him away from plans the two of you had already made."

"No problem," she said, waving it off despite another pang. "I'm glad to see him doing something fun, and I'm sure he'll enjoy the game with you more than some stuffy old gallery."

"You were going to the Bernard showing?"

Surprised, Alex nodded. "Yes. You've heard of the artist?"

"I own two of her originals."

She stared, agape. "How...interesting." Interesting? More like "astounding."

A light rap sounded at her open door. "Ms. Tremont?"

Alex looked up to see one of the fine jewelry salesclerks. "Yes, Carla?"

"I brought the wedding ring sets you requested."

She motioned her inside. "Excuse me, Jack, this will just take a moment." Alex lifted the lid on one of the two cigar-box-size jeweler's cases, and smiled her pleasure at the dazzling array of gold, platinum and white-gold sets of wedding bands. "Yes, Carla, these are the exact cases I was interested in. Thank you."

Carla left and Alex set aside the open box, noting Jack's pallor. She swallowed a smile, thinking maybe she shouldn't tell him she was considering having him wear some of them in the commercial shoots Monday.

"Have you ever been married, Jack?"

"No."

The one clipped word, along with his shifted gaze, told her volumes. If the mere sight of the rings made the man that nervous, she would skip them. There was something to be said about portraying Jack as the free-spirited bachelor he was. After all, she had certainly found it appealing, hadn't she?

But art collector? She opened her mouth to inquire into this most intriguing bit of information, but her father returned to claim Jack for their afternoon at the stadium. Feeling like a little girl being left behind, Alex followed them to the doorway of her office and leaned against the frame. Hugging herself, she watched Jack as he walked away, talking easily with her intimidating father, and wondered how many other layers this man had to reveal.

But her musings were derailed when Heath appeared in the hallway, walking toward her father and Jack. Her pulse stalled for the few seconds the men conversed, and she experienced the strangest sensation when Jack and Heath shook hands. Engaged to one, fooling around with the other.

And what did that make *her?* Alex exhaled a shaky breath as several unflattering adjectives whirled through her mind. Her engagement ring winked at her, mocking her. She couldn't simply dismiss her betrayal to Heath—she needed to talk to him, the sooner, the better.

Heath gestured to the men's backs when he walked up, fresh-faced and unaware of her turmoil. "I thought you and Al were taking in the gallery today."

"We were."

He scoffed. "He stood you up for a lousy football game?"

"Yes."

"Well, you know I'm not much on this Bernard guy's art, but I'll go with you," he offered.

"She." A feeling of loss stabbed her as the two men walked onto the elevator and the door closed behind them.

"Excuse me?"

Alex looked back to Heath. "Bernard—the artist is a 'she.'"

Heath shrugged. "Whatever. Do you still want to go?"

She visualized giving back his ring, a teary goodbye. "Um, no," she said, suddenly changing her mind. "I think I'll take some flowers out to my mother's grave this afternoon." She needed the comfort of being close to someone who had loved her unconditionally. Perhaps she could sort out all of the mess in her head in the serenity of the shady cemetery.

As expected, Heath backed off immediately, even as he followed her into her office. "I'll let you have some private time, then. Hey, what's with the wedding rings?"

Alex sat in her comfy leather seat and unzipped the portfolio Jack had left, eager to see his new drawings. "I'm trying to work the rings into the new ad campaign."

"Hmm. Any of these you like well enough for me to wear?"

Her head jerked up when his words sank in. "What?"

"Why not?" Heath said, gesturing to the rings. "We've put this off long enough, don't you think?"

14

"WHAT DID YOU SAY?" Lana asked.

Alex sighed into the phone and hooked her legs over the arm of her faithful chair. "I agreed to go away with Heath next weekend to talk about where our relationship goes from here. His timing is uncanny."

"Maybe he senses another buck sniffing around his doe."

"Oh, now that's romantic. If you don't buy the coffee shop, maybe you should start writing greeting cards for a living." At the sound of a distant *ping*, she turned her head toward the balcony door. Seeing nothing, she dismissed the noise. "Any big Sunday plans?"

"I'm working this afternoon. How about you?"

"Cleaning, I guess. Heath left again this morning for Cincinnati. How's your roommate situation?"

"Intolerable. We're not even speaking now, we leave notes. I write mine in pig Latin just to piss her off."

Ping. Alex frowned at the noise, standing this time. "Hold on, Lana, I think I hear something."

"What?"

Ping.

"I don't know." She moved toward the glass door and slid it open just in time for a pea-sized pebble to bounce off her forehead. "Ow!"

"What happened?"

"I have to go."

"Don't leave me hanging—"

Alex disconnected the call and stepped out onto her balcony, barely dodging another pebble before she leaned over the railing.

Jack stood on the ground, two stories below, one hand pulled back in preparation to launch another pebble, the other loaded with enough ammo to pester her for a week. He stopped when he saw her and gave her a boyish grin.

Alex's spirits lifted absurdly. "You almost gave me a concussion," she yelled.

"That's my secret weapon," he yelled back. "Women with concussions are much easier to persuade."

Wary, she crossed her arms. She couldn't imagine what the man might say that would provide the slightest bit of enticement. "Persuade to do what?"

He held up two pink slips of paper. "Tickets to the Bernard showing this afternoon."

Okay, she was enticed.

"Including a reception for the artist."

Alex pursed her mouth. "I...need to change."

He grinned. "Wear riding clothes. The weather is great."

Telling herself that *this* was not a date, this was *not* a date, and this was not a *date*, Alex scoured her wardrobe for something casual and funky. She settled on a pair of black corduroy overalls, a heavy silk coral long-sleeve blouse, and suede slip-ons with a heavy sole. She dumped the contents of her leather tote into a hand appliquéd canvas bag, then dropped in a handful of hairpins so she could twist back her helmet hair once she reached the gallery. At the last minute, she remembered his leather jacket and grabbed it on the way out the door.

Telling herself she was hurrying because Jack was waiting rather than because she was excited, Alex jogged down the hall, slowing when she reached the corridor before Lana's apartment. Hopes that she would make it past without notice were dashed when she rounded the corner to find Lana leaning in her open doorway, filing her nails.

"Got a date?" her friend asked innocently without lifting her gaze.

Alex sighed. "It's not a date. Jack is taking me to the Bernard art show that Dad and I missed yesterday so they could go to a football game."

"Mmm-hmm. One man, one woman, and a place to go. Sounds like a date to me."

"It's not a date," she insisted. "We both happen to have an interest in this artist, that's all."

Lana glanced up. "Jack the Attack is a contemporary art connoisseur?"

"He has two Bernard originals."

Her friend stopped filing. "For real?"

Alex pursed her mouth and nodded.

"Holy husband-hunting, Alex, I'm starting to think there's more to this man than meets the eye—and what meets the eye isn't too shabby."

She shook her finger. "Oh, no, don't read anything into this. We're going to an art gallery, and that's all."

Lana shrugged. "Okay. Just remember you're supposed to set a wedding date this weekend—to marry a different man." She blew on her nails, then stepped inside and closed the door with her hip.

Alex shook her head, then turned toward the exit, although her steps were somewhat more hesitant.

This was not a date.

"SO, JACK, WHO'S YOUR DATE?"

Alex nearly choked on her champagne, but extended her hand when Jack introduced her to Bernard Penn, the artist whom she'd admired since the woman's first Lexington show nearly six years ago. Jack explained that his father had mentored the unknown local artist before she moved on to make her name in Chicago and Los Angeles. From the looks the quirky young woman was giving Jack, Alex wondered if he himself had mentored her in other areas.

"Jack gave me my first tattoo," Bernard announced, pointing to her bikini area, confirming Alex's suspicions.

"A trade for one of her paintings," Jack added.

"Made you earn the other one, too," the young woman said slyly before moving on to mingle.

Alex lifted her eyebrows over her champagne glass. "Just how large *is* your art collection?"

A slow grin spread over Jack's face. "I stopped counting canvases in ninety-three. Come with me. There's a piece in the atrium I'd like to show you." He clasped her hand and she didn't pull away, casting sideways glances at him as they walked, marveling at how comfortable he seemed in a cultural environment, and how little she actually knew about him.

"Where is your collection?" she asked.

"My place." They moved into the atrium, and Jack pointed out an abstract of musical instruments, commenting on the composition, the striking use of color and light.

"Nice," she said, nodding. "Where do you live?"

"Derek and I turned an older home in Lansdowne into a duplex, but since he and his wife will be needing more space, I'm giving him my side when they return from their honeymoon."

"That's generous of you."

He shook his head. "Derek has carried my weight around the agency more than once. He's a good man, and it's the least I can do."

"So where will you live?"

He shrugged. "I'll find a place—I mainly use the duplex as storage for my art collection."

Alex angled her head. "So you weren't kidding about having a large collection that you, um, traded for?"

Jack nodded and gave her a crooked smile. "Not in the

way you think, though. I've traveled a lot and picked up local pieces for a few bucks, and I've bartered an odd job here and there."

"I'd like to see it sometime," she murmured.

He shrugged. "Why not now?"

"I wasn't fishing for an invitation," she said, averting her gaze and extracting her hand from his.

Jack laughed. "I didn't think you were. Let's go. But I have to warn you, the place isn't exactly a penthouse loft."

She hesitated. The thought of going to his place seemed much too intimate in light of their recent encounter. "I shouldn't," she said, shaking her head. She didn't realize she was fingering her engagement ring until his gaze cut to her hand.

"Still wearing that thing?" he asked lightly.

Her defenses rallied. "Yes."

He made a sympathetic noise. "I never understood the allure of marriage myself."

"Call me old-fashioned," she said, lifting her chin. "But I like the idea of spending the rest of my life with one person."

One side of his mouth drew back. "Okay, Ms. Old-Fashioned, humor me. Let me show off my art collection to someone who actually knows a little bit about the art world."

"I'm sure I don't have your eye, or your expertise," she protested.

"Really? Did you select the Lenux hanging in your bathroom?"

She nodded.

"I have the companion piece."

"You're joking."

"Nope."

"What is it?"

"Come and see for yourself," he urged.

The knowledge that they shared an interest in the same artists left her absurdly pleased. And she had to admit, she was curious to see the man's living space. "Just a tour?"

He held up his hands. "Just a tour. We'll leave whenever you want to."

She wavered.

His eyes sobered. "Alex, I don't have an ulterior motive here to get you alone."

Alex squirmed, feeling foolish.

Jack pressed his lips together, then shifted his weight to his other foot. "I'm sorry our...mistake...Friday night left you in such an awkward position with your fiancé. We both got a little carried away." His color heightened, but his expression remained serious. "And Reddinger won't hear anything from me about what happened."

Alex exhaled, feeling relieved but also a little foolish for thinking that just because they would be alone, they would end up in bed again. Jack seemed as contrite as she about their lapse. They were adults who had learned from their "mistake." Besides, she suspected that for a man like Jack, the lure ended with the conquest. She was safe now. "Let's go," she agreed.

His grin buoyed her, sounding a little alarm in the back of her mind, which Alex ignored.

"Hungry?" he asked.

"A little."

"We can grab some fish sandwiches to go on the way. Sound good?"

She nodded, caught up in his excitement.

"Great. Let's ride."

During the drive across town, Alex tried to concentrate on the sweet-scented autumn air and the delicate orange and yellow leaves that swirled around them, but her senses were keen, making her ultra-aware of Jack's flat stomach muscles moving beneath her hands, of her thighs cradling his, her sex cupped against his buttocks. She told herself that once they arrived at his place, she'd maintain a room's distance from the man. At last he wheeled into the driveway of a large flagstone ranch home, and shut off the engine.

"I think you were more relaxed today," he teased as they removed their helmets.

She smiled, remembering her drive back from the cemetery yesterday, top down, hair flying. She hadn't reached any monumental conclusions during her trip, but she'd felt a little better upon returning. "It's kind of fun once you get the hang of it."

After they stowed their helmets and retrieved the bag of sandwiches, she followed Jack to a side entrance. The grass needed to be mowed, but its deep emerald color was a pleasing background for jewel-toned leaves that had settled around the base of trees and the house itself.

Jack moved casually, obviously much more at ease than she. After opening an aged beveled glass door, he swept his arm for her to precede him. Thrumming with curiosity, Alex stepped inside.

They entered through a tiny retro kitchen with hardwood floors, charming red tile counters, and white porcelain fixtures. And while the room was stripped bare of furniture and bric-a-brac, she received an immediate introduction to his art collection. Paintings of all sizes, framed and unframed, lined every inch of the anchor wall from floor to ceiling, stretching into a hallway beyond her vision. No theme or color scheme was observed, but each of the pieces was intriguing—landscapes, portraits, abstracts.

"Let's eat outside," he suggested. "Then I'll give you the full tour."

He retrieved a couple of beers from the refrigerator, then elbowed his way through a glass door that led to a brick patio in the backyard. Alex followed, admiring the simple wood table and chairs, also littered with bright leaves. Jack set their food and drinks on the table, then cleared a chair for her and raised the faded green umbrella to shield them from the sun.

"Thank you for taking me to the gallery," she said as they unwrapped the sandwiches.

He passed her an open bottle of beer. "It was the least I could do for taking your father away from you Saturday."

Alex bit into her sandwich and attempted a carefree shrug. "My father is free to spend his time as he pleases."

He dragged a French fry through a mound of ketchup. "You don't have to pretend. I enjoyed spending time with my old man, too. I would have been disappointed if I'd been in your shoes."

She smiled sadly. "It's easier with sons. Dad and I don't seem to be able to connect."

"Except at work?"

Surprised by his interest, she nodded. "Even though we don't always see eye to eye, it's the one passion we share."

He drank from his beer and settled back in his chair. The off-white shirt he wore looked crisp and new, and suited his coloring. The rolled up sleeves revealed his thick forearms. The man seemed comfortable in any setting. Part of her envied his nonchalance, his ability to move through life on his own terms.

"Alex, is the company really your passion?" he asked. "Or are you simply doing what you think your father expects of you?"

Although rankled, she tried to laugh. "That's a ridiculous question."

"Is it?"

"Yes," she insisted, then focused on removing the label from the cold bottle in one piece. "I mean, maybe at first I wanted to be close to Dad, but now..." She glanced up and sighed. "Well, I've come to realize that Dad doesn't care or even seem to notice how much I do at the store, so now I work strictly for my own fulfillment."

"I'm sure Al loves you very much," Jack said, his voice gentle.

She gave him a wry smile. "So much so that he'd rather spend time with you, a virtual stranger, than his own daughter." Her heart lurched. "You don't know how many times I've wished I'd been a boy."

Jack leaned forward, his mouth curving wide. "If I may say so, what a terrible waste *that* would have been."

She appreciated his attempt to lighten the mood and tingled under his compliment. "I probably sound like a spoiled little girl."

"Not at all," he assured her. "You must have been close to your mother."

"Yes," she murmured. "I suppose most children gravitate more toward one parent."

"I agree. I was closer to my father."

"You miss him." Not a question, because she knew he must.

Jack's smile didn't reach his eyes. "Every day that the sun rises."

So honest, she thought, shaken by his decidedly un-macho topic of conversation.

"But," he added, lifting his beer. "I'm fortunate to have some of Dad's canvases to remember him by. Let's finish up here so I can give you that tour."

His grin restored the cheerful atmosphere. They polished off their food in between discussing details for the commercial shoot the following day. Considering the strange way her body reacted every time she looked across the table at Jack—whom she was beginning to see in a new light—she decided to stick to neutral subjects like the ad campaign.

After discarding the leftovers, they carried their half-full bottles of beer back into the house. With her heart thumping in anticipation, Alex followed Jack slowly from room to room as he commented on the multitude of canvases and pointed out particular favorites of his, especially his father's. Because the rooms were void of furniture, they were free to walk around and admire each one. In one room which was obviously meant to be a small dining room, dozens of canvases were stacked and leaning against one wall.

"My vault," he offered.

"Jack," she breathed, afraid to touch anything, but wanting to see every piece. "You have enough work here to fill a small museum."

His smile was modest. "Maybe I'll open one when I'm old and gray. Meanwhile, I'll have to put them in storage."

She was struck by the simplicity of his life. A worn couch and chair in the living room, along with a nice stereo system, represented most of the furniture in his house. If he owned a television, it was hidden. A thin layer of dust covered everything, and the air was a little stale. The man was not fastidious—quite a contrast to Heath's compulsively clean, white decor. It was clear Jack spent his money on art, not trappings. And she suspected that over the years he had amassed a collection worth a small fortune.

The last room they came to was his bedroom. Alex hovered in the doorway and tingled as she scrutinized his intimate space, silently admiring the simple lines of the walnut bed and matching dresser, trying to ignore the rumpled nondescript comforter that covered his body at night. Again, canvases claimed every available space on the walls, and were stacked on the floor.

"Is this your easel?" she asked, stepping inside for a closer look at the wooden piece sitting next to the dresser.

"No, it was my father's."

She swallowed at the catch in his throat. "Do you paint?"

He smiled. "No. Unfortunately, I don't have my father's great talent."

"I looked over the drawings you left yesterday—they're quite wonderful."

He seemed pleased, but shook his head. "My work is strictly commercial grade. Besides, I'd rather collect. An artist can become too consumed with his own work to fully appreciate the work of others."

She regarded him, his long, lean frame draped casually in the doorway. An educated, charismatic man who seemed at ease in a corporate boardroom, but preferred to work at his small family advertising agency. An ex-jock who rode a motorcycle, but collected art. She smiled, shaking her head. "You are full of surprises, Jack Stillman."

His eyes changed, and his lips parted, and in a split second the atmosphere changed from comfortably friendly to sexually charged. Her body softened and warmed, and with jarring clarity, she remembered what it was like to be made love to by this man. She panicked, her breath catching when she realized that she wanted him to touch her again. At a loss, she turned her back, feigning fascination in the etching on the dresser mirror.

"Alex." He was behind her, pulling her hair away from her neck.

"Jack," she whispered, leaning back into him. "We shouldn't."

"I know." But the warm succulent kiss he lowered to the curve of her neck sent blood pooling to her breasts and thighs. His erection hardened against the swell of her hip as he reached around to cup her breasts. "I can't help myself," he said. "I want you, Alex." She moaned and lay her head back against his chest, undulating against him.

Within seconds he had unfastened her overalls and freed the buttons of her blouse, exposing her coral-colored lace bra. He pulled down the bra to expose the globes of her breasts, the hardened tips aching for attention. He nipped at her earlobe as he squeezed the pink peaks, mimicking the pressure, layering the sensations until Alex was writhing against him.

"Look at you, you're so beautiful," he murmured into her hair.

Their reflection riveted her, his hands large and tanned against her creamy skin. Desire buckled her knees, and she knew she was lost. "Jack...make love to me."

He groaned against her neck and slid his hand down over her bare stomach and inside her panties. The movement also served to strip her of the overalls, which she stepped out of, opening herself to Jack's fingers. As he plied her wetness, she reached behind her to tug at his clothing, which led to a frenzy of undressing. When they were both nude, Jack donned protection, then leaned into her from behind, grazing her sensitivity with his erection, whispering how much he wanted her. Already weak with wanting, Alex was riveted to the mirror that reflected their movements from the waist up.

White skin and brown, swollen breasts and big hands, narrow waist and broad shoulders, their bodies complemented each other perfectly, moving in synch, grazing sexes until their passion reached a fever pitch. "Now, Jack," she whispered, wild for the length of him inside her.

He lifted her until she half lay on the dresser for support, then probed her wetness before sliding inside.

"Ahh," he breathed, harmonizing with her moans. Every nerve ending sang as he began to make love to her with deep foraging thrusts. Emotions flitted over his face—need, pain, pleasure. She gave in to the sawing rhythm he set, and her climax burst around her with shocking haste. Amidst the blinding, delicious shock waves, she was aware that he, too, had surrendered to a quick, powerful release, evident by his contracted muscles, guttural moans and intense expressions.

Slowly, slowly, they recovered together. Alex sucked in a

sharp breath when he withdrew and lowered her to her feet. He was gentle, making sure she could support her weight before he released her. They dressed in silence, the snaps and scrapes of various fasteners sounding loud in the acoustics of awkwardness.

Alex welcomed the sting of remorse when it hit her, but she didn't waste time berating herself—she'd known what she was doing, knew the ramifications of another encounter with Jack. In for a penny, in for a pound. Indeed, with every look they'd exchanged today, she'd felt herself growing farther from Heath, and closer to Jack. Her desire for him was so great, the certain dead end of the road she was traveling seemed not to matter. She'd never felt more out of control in her life—her newly discovered capacity for self-indulgence scared her to death.

"I—" She jumped at the sound of her own voice. "I think you'd better take me home, Jack."

She wanted him to object, to give her some indication that their fast and furious lovemaking meant more to him than a simple score, but he simply nodded, his expression unreadable.

During the agonizing ride across town, Alex felt worse and worse. She tried to hold on while maintaining as much distance between their bodies as possible. By the time they reached her building, however, Alex had recovered enough to realize it was up to her to repair their working relationship, if possible. After all, tomorrow was the all-important commercial and photo shoot—they'd be together for several hours.

When he stopped the motorcycle, she slid off the bike quickly and unstrapped her helmet as he killed the engine. Dusk was beginning to settle, and his face was swathed in gray shadow.

"Jack—"

"Alex—"

They both stopped and smiled awkwardly.

"Can we just—"

"—forget what happened?"

Alex swallowed, then nodded. "That would be best. My God, I'm engaged and you're..."

"Happily single," he supplied with a wry grin. "Alex, I'm incredibly attracted to you, but you're right—we're moving in opposite directions here. I'm sorry if this has complicated things for you and..."

"Heath," she supplied. "That's none of your concern, Jack." Her tone was more abrupt than she meant it to be, but Jack didn't need to know her plans regarding her compromised engagement. Inhaling deeply, she attempted to change the subject, and the mood. "Thanks again for taking me to the gallery. And for sharing your collection." Other things they'd shared leapt to her mind.

"You're welcome."

Silence stretched between them for several seconds before he said, "I'll see you tomorrow at the studio."

She nodded as she backed away. After a short wave, she turned and, despite her urge to run, managed to walk calmly to the stairwell. But as soon as she was out of sight, she broke into a jog, hating the tears that burned her eyes. Humiliation washed over her in waves as she recalled the incident—humiliation not because she'd once again had sex with Jack, but because she'd enjoyed it. Reveled in it, even.

After slipping into her apartment, she sat in the dark for a few seconds, wondering how her life had swerved so out of control in the past few days. She missed her mother's counsel, and she wished she felt close enough to discuss private matters with her father. Besides, she was all grown up, and vying for a vice presidency—why couldn't she sort out something so simple as her taboo attraction to a rebellious playboy?

Ping.

Alex looked over at the sliding glass window and waited for the second pebble to make its mark before she walked outside to lean over the balcony railing, crazily cheered. "You're determined to break something, aren't you?"

The white of his teeth flashed in the near-darkness. "Sorry to bother you," Jack called up, "but I wanted to say..."

"Yes?" she asked, her heart thumping.

"That I hope Reddinger knows what a lucky man he is."

Stunned into speechlessness, she could only stare as he waved, then climbed onto his bike and drove away.

15

"SORRY I'VE BEEN TRAVELING so much lately," Heath said over the phone. "Do you have a busy day planned?"

Alex doodled on a notepad on her desk, jumpy and miserable, wanting desperately to find comfort in Heath's voice. This was the man who cared about her, the man who shared her views and her values, the man who wanted to marry her. And didn't she want someone to be close to? Someone to grow old with?

Yes, more than anything.

But she'd jeopardized her chance for a trusting, long-term relationship by indulging in foolishness with Jack Stillman. Now what?

Alex tried to sound as normal as possible, despite her teeming unrest. "This afternoon is the commercial and photo shoot."

"That was pretty quick scheduling," Heath said.

"Jack knows the producer, some guy named Richardson. He pulled a couple of strings to get the studio time and, frankly, I'd just as soon get it over with."

"Well, the man will be in his element."

His tone picked at her tangled nerves. "What do you mean?"

Heath scoffed. "He's a natural performer. He knows how to manipulate people to get what he wants out of them—sympathy, admiration, a job."

She bristled at the idea that she was just another person

taken in by Jack's undeniable charisma. "Funny, but he strikes me as being a very genuine person."

"Alex," he said, his voice colored with irritation, "I would expect this naiveté from Al, but not from you."

"Naiveté?"

"Come on, Alex, he's been working the two of you from the beginning. Al swallowed his bait hook, line and sinker, but I thought you were more objective. I wouldn't put it past this guy to try to make a pass at you."

Alex swallowed hard. "I think you're giving him a little too much credit."

"Being a con man is a gift. Just be glad he can put his talent to good use for Tremont's in front of the camera."

Funny, she didn't feel glad. And the feeling of nongladness lasted throughout the morning, her mood matching the lousy weather as black clouds rolled in from the west. Heath's words ran over and over through her head. She'd suspected from the beginning that Jack was playing her father, yet somewhere along the way, she had fallen under his spell, too. Was it his plan all along to seduce her for leverage? And how easily had she played into his hands?

Confused and fidgety, Alex reviewed everything she knew about Jack Stillman, beginning with her first visit to his dilapidated office. He'd told her and everyone else that he'd arranged the conditions purposefully to set up his presentation the next day. She hadn't believed him, but neither had she called his bluff. Perhaps another look at his operations would resurrect all those doubts which had kept her objective and sharp in the beginning. And did she ever need some objectivity.

She glanced at her watch, noting the time she'd have to leave for the studio. But since Jack's mode of transportation would be hampered by the ominous weather, she'd simply leave early and pick him up at his office on the way to the studio. Maybe the stark reminder of his less-than-stellar enterprise would give her a badly needed dose of reality.

Jack Stillman would never be the kind of man she wanted and needed in her life.

JACK CONSIDERED TAKING A CAB to the office Monday morning, but decided the short ride in the driving rain might clear his head of tormenting visions of Alex and their extraordinary lovemaking.

Was he ever wrong.

He arrived at the office around nine-fifteen, soaked, and chagrined to see that Tuesday's and Stripling's cars were both there.

"You're late," Tuesday announced when he opened the door and walked in, dripping.

He removed his leather jacket and shot her an annoyed glance. "I almost drowned getting here, thanks for your concern."

"Don't shake that wet coat in here," she warned. "And my only concern is collecting my money for Friday's daily double."

"Got it right here," he assured her, tossing the coat in the hallway corner, then closing the door. Jack withdrew an envelope, and handed it to Tuesday. "Twelve hundred fifty-five dollars. Pretty good wages for a job that doesn't exist."

She opened the envelope for a quick peek, then sniffed. "I'm worth twice as much," she said, then nodded toward the back. "Tax man's here, a quaking nervous wreck that you didn't bet his horse to place like he told you."

Jack wheeled to walk to the back office, and crashed through a set of black swinging saloon doors that hadn't been there before. He turned around and walked back through to the front office. "What, may I ask, are these?"

"I decided I need my privacy up here," Tuesday said,

stuffing her money deep into the neckline of her dress. "The doors break up the space properlike."

Actually, they looked pretty darn good. "Where did you get the doors?"

"Found them in the Dumpster," Tuesday said. "Slapped a coat of paint on them, and they're as good as new. Marion helped me hang them this morning."

"Marion?" Jack's eyebrows shot straight up. "After nearly crippling the man, you're on a first-name basis?"

"He's feeling much better. I gave him another adjustment last night, and he threw away the board."

"Last night?" Jack asked, then held up his hand. "Wait, I don't want to know." Sounded as though everyone was having success in the romance department except him.

He pushed through the doors again into the back office where Stripling sat, sipping tea, and looking as limber as a willow switch. Tuesday followed him.

"Well?" The man's Adam's apple bobbed. "Did you bet the horse to place? I saw in the paper that she won, and the payout was pretty good."

Making a sympathetic sound, Jack shook his head. "No, Stripling, I didn't bet the horse to place like you told me."

The man's thin shoulders fell.

Jack grinned and whipped out another envelope. "I bet her to win! Seventy-five dollars for a two dollar bet, and I put your entire hundred on her."

Stripling's jaw opened and closed as he lunged for the envelope. "Oh, my goodness! Oh, my goodness!"

"Oh, my goodness is right," Tuesday mumbled, frowning. "If that horse had come in second instead of first, you would have lost his money."

"But if I had bet the horse to come in second—"

"—like he *told* you to—"

"—the payout wouldn't have been as good." He shrugged. "What can I say? I was feeling lucky."

"And just how much did *you* pocket?" she asked.

"Well," Jack drawled as he pulled out the last fat envelope. "I hate to brag, but I cleared just under five gees."

Stripling whistled low. "You're going to have to claim that money on your personal income tax form, you know."

Jack frowned in his direction, then his attention was diverted by the opening of the front door. When had Tuesday hung a bell on it to announce visitors?

"That must be the furniture," Tuesday sang, then strode toward the front.

A few seconds passed before her words sank it. "Furniture?" Jack croaked. "What furniture?"

He jogged to the front just as a huge man in a yellow slicker walked in, holding a clipboard and directing two young men who had a desk hoisted on their shoulders.

"You Stillman?" the man asked.

"Yes. What's this all about?"

The man sucked his teeth, then read from the clipboard. "I got an order here for two desks, two file cabinets and two leather chairs. That'll be three thousand, two hundred dollars, cash on delivery."

"What?" Jack's temples nearly exploded. "I didn't order all this stuff." He whirled to Tuesday. "Did *you* do this?"

She blinked, her face innocent. "I distinctly remember you saying Friday that you were going to win enough money to buy the new equipment the agency needed."

"But...but I didn't mean— Hey, watch that leather coat in the hallway, buddy!"

Tuesday snatched the envelope out of his hand and counted bills as she talked. "The Salvation Army will be here in a few minutes to pick up the old furniture, so it'll be out of the way by the time the computers arrive."

"Computers?" Jack asked wearily.

"My daughter-in-law works at a computer store across

town—I got you a great deal." She handed him the balance of the money, along with two aspirins and a cup of water.

Jack swallowed the pills dry. "Tuesday," he said, holding on to the wall for support. "Did it occur to you to ask me first?"

"No," she said matter-of-factly. "Because it's my job to get things organized around here."

He thought he might pass out—Derek certainly would when he found out. "There...is...no...*job!*"

ALEX WAS GRATEFUL the showers had subsided enough for her to dash from the store van into the building that housed the Stillman & Sons Advertising Agency. With a rueful shake of her head, she remembered coming here only last week, marveling at the whirlwind of events that had taken place since. Had she really known Jack for only a few days? Odd, but the man had plowed a disruptive furrow through her life that bespoke a much longer relationship than existed. And a much more meaningful one.

Shaking off her wayward thoughts, she retraced her steps down the hall, noting that at least the carpet had been cleaned, and the sour, mildewed smell was gone. When she twisted the doorknob, she noticed that the agency sign had been repaired. And when she stepped inside, the transformation was nothing short of remarkable—furniture, plants, music, *cleanliness.* A matronly black woman turned from a file cabinet and flashed a friendly smile. "Now you must be Ms. Tremont."

Alex blinked because she hadn't called ahead. "Um, yes. Have we met?"

"I just knew it from Mr. Stillman's description of you," the woman said. "I'm Tuesday, the agency's office manager."

"Pleased to meet you," she said, extending her hand. The agency must be rebounding if they had hired an office manager. And purchased new furniture. And cleaned. "I should have called—Mr. Stillman isn't expecting me. Considering the weather, I thought I might give him a ride to the television station."

"Well, now that's mighty nice of you," the woman said, beaming. She gestured toward a love seat, covered with a lush moss-green velvet. "Won't you have a seat? I'll let Mr. Stillman know you're here. Would you like some hot tea?"

Alex took the proffered seat and nodded dumbly. "Yes, please."

"Cream and sugar?"

"Both, please."

The woman disappeared through a set of swinging half-doors that she didn't remember. She heard the rumble of at least one male voice, maybe two. A couple of minutes later, the office manager emerged, bearing a cup and saucer. "Here's your tea. Mr. Stillman is on a conference call with a client, but I let him know you were here, so I'm sure he'll be right out."

"Thank you." On a conference call with a client? She just assumed he was spending all his time on the Tremont's account, but he had mentioned doing business with Phillips' Honey, and after all, his brother was still out of town. Alex picked up the cup and smiled. "What extraordinary china."

Tuesday smiled. "Mr. Stillman insists on nice little touches around here."

The black doors swung out and an older man appeared. "Tuesday," he said, "do you have time for lunch?"

The woman shook her head mournfully. "The phones have been ringing off the hook around here, I'd better not."

So they were busy, Alex thought, sipping her very tasty tea.

"Want me to pick up something for you?"

Tuesday passed on his offer, and when the man left, Alex asked, "That wasn't the other Mr. Stillman, was it?"

"No, that's Mr. Stripling. He only comes in when it gets really crazy around here."

Alex pursed her mouth. Darn—the agency *was* busy. And so different, she found it hard to believe things could have changed so much in a week's time. Was it possible that Jack *had* set her up that first day to lay a foundation for his presentation? "Tuesday, how long have you worked for the agency?"

The woman looked heavenward. "Can't rightly say how long I've been working here—seems like forever."

"And has the office always looked like this?"

"Ever since I've been here." Then she smiled. "Oh, you're talking about that day Mr. Stillman was trying to get your goat." She laughed, slapping her thigh. "That man and his elaborate schemes."

Alex's mouth fell open.

Tuesday's face shone with affection. "Yes, he's a rebel, that one, but it worked, didn't it?"

She couldn't believe it—layers just *kept* peeling off the man.

"My ears are burning," Jack said, strolling in and turning his full-fledged grin toward Alex.

Alex swallowed hard. Funny—just the sight of him set every part of her aflame. "Um, hi. I came by to...um..." Darn it, why *had* she come by?

"To make sure you weren't late to the studio," Tuesday supplied, then disappeared through the swinging doors.

"Right," she parroted, feeling all of twelve years old. Standing, she experienced a bad premonition about the commercial shoot, but a second later she chided herself— she would be watching him from a distance—how dangerous could the man be across a room, surrounded by cameras and lights?

"Give me a minute," he said with a devilish wink, jerking his thumb toward his office. "I just need to grab my thong."

"ALEX," JACK SAID, "this is Sammy Richardson, producer here at the station and an old friend of mine."

Sammy Richardson was not only *not* a man, she was the most female woman Alex had ever seen. Alex suspected that if she'd been a male cartoon character, this would be the point where her eyeballs would bulge out of her head and drop on the floor. Sammy's long, long hair was a thousand shades of natural blond, and her skin was one shade of a natural golden glow. Stunning was the only word to describe her long, curvaceous body, magnificent in jeans and a man's shirt. Old friend? Yeah, right. "Hello," she managed to say. "I'm Alex Tremont."

"Nice to meet you." Sammy's handshake was firm, her gaze direct and friendly. "Perhaps we can talk about what you're looking for today while Jack goes to hair and makeup."

A frown crossed Jack's face, but he left with an assistant, grumbling. Alex followed Sammy to a makeshift desk a few feet away from a myriad of sets surrounded by cameras and lights. "Okay, let's talk about the shoot," she said without preliminaries. "My people will be here in a half hour, ready to start."

Alex opened her notebook. "Tremont's is considering hiring Jack Stillman as a spokesman."

"Good decision," the woman interjected smoothly.

Bristling at the woman's knowing tone, she said, "We're *considering* hiring Mr. Stillman. The outcome will depend on the success of this shoot."

"What mood are we going for here?"

She squirmed, pushing the tentative slogan across the table: Tremont's. Because clothes *do* make the man. "Um, you know...persuasive, compelling..."

"Sexy?" The woman's mouth curved into a catlike smile.

"Um, yes."

"Jack can certainly handle that assignment," Sammy murmured, seemingly a hundred miles away.

"Yes, he can." Alex agreed pleasantly, ridiculously tempted to let the woman know that she wasn't the only one in the room who knew the particulars of Jack's carnal skills. When she realized how trampy that sounded, she clamped her mouth shut, mentally kicking herself. Trying to steer the conversation back to business, she withdrew a folder of the reduced images Jack had presented at the first meeting, along with a storyboard. "The two female models I requested from the agency we use should be here soon."

Sammy's eyebrows rose. "Just two? Jack *has* settled down."

Alex frowned. "Building on Jack's original ideas, I'd like to focus on four settings—the gym, the backyard barbecue, the office, and the, um, bedroom."

The woman nodded, making notes fast and furious. "Let me call props with this list, and we'll be good to go as soon as Jack is ready and the models get here."

Alex studied the woman while she spoke on the phone, a little awed by her sparkling beauty. Sammy and Jack would make a spectacular-looking couple, she acknowledged, wondering how recently they'd been involved and why their relationship hadn't worked. And her stomach felt strange at the thought of them together.

Sammy hung up the phone and smiled broadly. "The props will be here in ten minutes. Let's take a look at the sets."

"So," Alex ventured as they picked their way around the equipment, "you and Jack go way back."

"Oh, yeah," the woman said. "Way back. We even lived together for a while, but I wanted to get married."

"Oh." Alex paused for casual effect. "And he didn't?"

Sammy laughed, a melodious sound. "Jack? The man is a rolling stone—he'll never commit to anything or anyone. I was astounded when he told me he was working at the agency again." She laughed. "Wonder how long that will last?"

"Long enough to handle our account, hopefully," Alex said, irritated.

"Oh, Derek will take care of you," she said with a dismissive wave. "He's the dependable one. Just be thankful you nailed down Jack long enough for these photos." She shook her head and made a regretful sound. "He used to get offers all the time to model, do sports commentary, endorsements. Could have made a boatload of money."

"He didn't want the money?" Alex asked, dropping all pretense of disinterest.

"He didn't want the responsibility," Sammy corrected. "I told you—the man is commitment-shy. He'll work just long enough to fund his freedom."

"You sound a little bitter," Alex said quietly.

The woman shook her head. "I'm not. Jack didn't deceive me. He told me up front that he didn't ever plan to marry, but I thought I could change his mind." She turned, one eyebrow lifted. "When I look back, though, the one thing I appreciate most about Jack is that he's honest." Then she laughed. "Well, maybe there are one or two other things."

Alex squirmed.

"Hey," the woman said, suddenly serious, her gaze direct. "I'm only telling you this to keep you from making the same mistake I made."

Attempting nonchalance, Alex said, "You're wrong if you think—"

"I know what I see," Sammy said, her voice gentle but firm.

Jack entered from the side, wearing a white bathrobe, flanked by two giggling young women who were still powdering his nose and patting his hair.

"See," the woman continued. "He's irresistible. Every

woman he meets falls in love with him. But believe me, don't do it. It took me years to get over him." Sammy clapped her hands to get the attention of the crew that appeared pushing pallets of furniture and other props, then started belting out directions.

Alex tried to shrug off the woman's well-meaning warning—she had nothing to worry about. But she found herself mesmerized as the shoot commenced and Jack moved through numerous takes like a pro.

He was gorgeously somber in the business suit scenes, striding with purpose across an office setting.

He was charmingly casual in the backyard barbecue scene, tending a grill.

He was breathtakingly sweaty in the gym scene, lifting weights.

And he was knee-weakeningly sexy in the bedroom scene, reclining in boxers, the hand of one of the models on his shoulder.

The photographer took rolls and rolls of film of him in every one of the outfits she'd chosen—including the black thong, which had all the women on the set twitching. Sammy suggested that they get a couple shots with his tattoo showing, which only heightened the mood.

The man was magic, Alex conceded, and the camera loved him. He moved with economy, somehow packing a sense of approachable masculinity into every gesture. Occasionally, he made eye contact with her, and to her consternation, her body leapt in response. After three hours of a slow-burn, Alex had to cross her legs.

Sammy threw her a sympathetic look, then yelled, "Cut—that's a wrap."

16

"LOOKS TO ME LIKE your business is just starting to gain some momentum," Stripling said, handing Jack a stack of papers. "So I'm recommending that the penalties and interest be dropped. Coupled with the payment plan I set up, the agency should be caught up on its back taxes within six months."

Jack shook his hand. "Thanks, Stripling. My brother Derek will be so relieved."

The man's smile was genuine. "Good luck, Jack." He tipped his hat to Tuesday, who gave him a fond wink.

When the door closed, Jack wheeled and pushed through the swinging doors. He poured himself another cup of coffee, then dropped into his new leather swivel chair in front of his new wood and metal desk. To his extreme aggravation, Tuesday was on his heels.

"All right, out with it."

Jack frowned. "What?"

"You just got the IRS off your back, you have six new client appointments set up for next week, your brother will be back in a few days to help, and I've never seen such a long face."

Jack drank deeply from his cup. Since Monday, he'd been battling a funk born of proximity to Alexandria Tremont. After the shoot was over, she'd announced she would be in touch once they had the results of the focus group audience, maybe sometime this week. After several days of regular contact with her, he supposed he was suffering from withdrawal. He found himself toying with the phone, or riding his bike near her building on the off chance a legitimate excuse for talking to her would occur to him. One didn't.

He simply couldn't get the woman out of his mind.

"It's that Tremont lady, isn't it?"

"Absolutely not."

"Whew, the fire alarm's going to go off for sure, 'cause liar, liar, your pants are on *fire*."

He rolled his eyes upward to meet her disapproving gaze. "I don't want to talk about it."

"Okay," she sang, throwing up her arms and turning toward the front office. "No one can accuse Tuesday Humphrey of sticking her nose in where it don't belong."

Jack snorted as she moved through the swinging doors, then swiveled his chair around to face the easels of posters he'd drawn for the Tremont's account. He'd lain awake most of the night exploring his state of mind, and trying to get to the root of the problem. He wished he'd never agreed to be the spokesman for the department store, account or no account. Because on top of the increasingly suffocating feeling of being tied to someone else's schedule, there was the little problem of working with Alex.

No, he corrected, the problem wasn't working with Alex—the problem was working with Alex and not being able to take her home afterward. He lusted after the woman with an unprecedented intensity, and he knew they could have fun together for a while. But Alex was engaged to a successful man, and he had nothing to offer her save a pile of paintings.

At the races she'd said she liked the serious, professional side of him. Except the serious, professional side of him that she'd seen had all been a sham, propped up by his lies and Tuesday's corroboration. He had no desire to be serious and professional. Just thinking about being tied to this desk, or to any desk, made him jittery.

What he needed was distance from her. Maybe if he took a trip, gave her time to marry Reddinger...

His phone beeped, which meant Tuesday had patched a call through to his line.

"Jack Stillman," he said into the handset.

"Jack, it's Al Tremont."

"Hey, Mr. T., what can I do for you?"

"Just calling with good news, son. The focus group gave the commercials a big thumbs-up, highest marks possible."

"That's great, sir."

"So, with that little formality behind us, we need to sit down and negotiate a long-term contract with your agency, and for you to be the exclusive Tremont's spokesman! The marketing department is gearing up for billboards, personal appearances, you name it."

Jack's stomach clenched. "Mr. T., I need to talk to you about that. Of course, the agency would be honored to handle your business, but...I'm bowing out as spokesman."

Al made a choking sound. "What? I don't understand."

"I'll honor the contract we signed giving Tremont's permission to use the spots that were filmed, but that's the end of it for me."

"But why, son?"

"It's complicated, sir."

"It's Alex, isn't it?"

Jack blinked. How much did her father know? "I don't know if you've talked to Alex about it—"

"Yes," Al cut in. "I know it puts you in an awkward situation, son, but I was hoping the two of you could work together despite the, um, *problem.*"

Damn, maybe they were closer than he'd assumed. "Please don't take offense, sir, but I simply can't work under these circumstances. I'll hand off your account to Derek, and I'm sure you'll find a new spokesperson soon."

Al cleared his throat with a low rumble. "I don't think

you understand, son. It's *you* I want, not your agency. I can get just about anyone to come up with a catchy slogan and draw me a few pictures, but I want Jack the Attack representing the store."

Stunned, Jack sat in silence. Just as he'd suspected.

"To put it plainly, Jack—no endorsement, no advertising account. And if it sweetens the pot a little, you won't be working with Alex. You'll be working with our new vice president of marketing and sales, Bobby Warner."

So Alex hadn't received the promotion.

"What do you say, Jack? Are you in?"

Jack sighed, and although anger drummed through his veins, he could imagine the disappointment on Derek's face when he told him they'd lost the account.

"Sure, Mr. T. I'm in."

SHE LOVED HIM. A person got a lot of thinking done in the course of three sleepless nights, and after dissecting Sammy Richardson's advice during the commercial shoot, Alex had come to a frightening conclusion. She, the woman who prided herself on forging a stable future on all fronts, had fallen for a motorcycle-riding rebel who would soon be voluntarily homeless and had no intention of settling down with one woman.

And with the overwhelmingly positive response from the focus group, it looked as if Jack would not only be their spokesman, but would be handling their advertising account to boot. She'd kept her word to her father, and although she'd underestimated Jack's ability, she was willing to concede that having him as a spokesman might give them the sales boost they needed.

She'd simply have to find a way to disguise her feelings for Jack and work with him until she could arrange to hand off the ad agency liaison responsibilities. The future seemed a little vague, but of one thing she was certain—when Heath returned from Cincinnati this afternoon, she would break their engagement.

Funny, how her feelings for him—or rather, her lack of feelings for him—now seemed so crystal clear relative to her feelings for Jack. She realized how much she and Heath had been robbing each other of a wonderful experience. Heath deserved someone who loved him the way she loved Jack—wildly and unreasonably. If Heath truly loved her, which, upon reflection of their relationship, she doubted, then he would eventually get over her, just as she would eventually get over Jack.

"Alex," her father said, striding into her office without the courtesy of a knock. His face was flushed scarlet, and she was immediately concerned for his health.

"Yes, Dad?"

"I just wanted you to know that you almost cost us an ace spokesman."

She frowned. "What do you mean?"

"I just got off the phone with Jack Stillman, and he was ready to decline a long-term contract for spokesman because he said he couldn't work with you anymore."

Confusion, hurt, anger—her mixed emotions, tripped her tongue. "I d-don't understand."

"You promised me," her father said, his tone low and accusing. "You promised me that you would work *with* him, and now I find out that you've been so difficult, he doesn't want to work with Tremont's at all."

Difficult? Because she'd slept with him? Did Jack now find the situation too awkward? Her mouth opened and closed, but no sound emerged.

"All because you were determined to sign some high and mighty advertising agency from St. Louis," he added.

"I had no idea Jack felt that way," she murmured, standing on shaky knees. "But if you feel so strongly about having Jack Stillman as spokesman—"

"You know I do!"

She swallowed. "I was planning to step aside and let someone else work with the ad agency."

"There's no need," her father said, laying a memo on her desk. "Bobby Warner was just named vice president of sales & marketing, and he'll be taking over those duties." He exited as he'd entered, without preamble.

Stunned, Alex sat down to read the memo, disappointment coursing through her. Stinging from her father's words and Jack's betrayal, she swung her chair around to face her computer, and put her fingers on the keyboard.

Through a blur of tears, she typed a short letter of resignation from the company she loved. Her father's attitude had made one thing perfectly clear—she could no longer work in this environment, yearning for the love of two men she'd never have.

A few minutes later, a knock sounded at her door. Sniffing quickly, Alex looked up to see Heath stick his head in. "I heard," he said softly. "Can I come in?"

She nodded, her stomach churning. "When did you get back?"

"Just now. I'm sorry about the vice presidency, Alex, but in light of my news, it might be for the best."

She frowned. "What news?"

His smile was a bit shaky. "One of the reasons I've been spending a lot of time in Cincinnati lately is because the bank where the store has its accounts has offered me a job. A great job."

Unable to hide her surprise, she asked, "Why haven't you said anything?"

He shrugged. "I was afraid it wouldn't pan out, and I didn't want you or your dad thinking I wasn't being loyal. I know this company means everything to you."

"Heath, I just typed my letter of resignation."

"What?" His expression changed from surprise to elation.

"That's wonderful! Now we can both go to Cincinnati—I know you'll be able to find a terrific job there, Alex."

She looked at Heath, his cheeks pink from excitement, his eyes shining with enthusiasm. They could make a clean break from Tremont's, from Lexington, from her father, from Jack. Could their relationship be salvaged?

Alex bit down hard on her lip, wavering.

17

TO GET HIS MIND OFF ALEX that afternoon, Jack threw himself into the paperwork on his desk, finishing tasks as fast as Tuesday could stack them in front of him.

"I don't know what's gotten into you," she said, finger wagging, "but I hope it's chronic."

Jack sighed. The *last* thing he needed was a persistent dose of the hots for Alex Tremont. "Would you mind labeling folders for the accounts we'll be calling on next week? I need to file some information I found on the Internet."

"One step ahead of you," she said cheerfully, setting the stack of labeled folders on the edge of his desk.

Jack smiled. "Thanks."

"Do you mind if I take off a little early? Reggie wants me to meet his girlfriend tonight, so he's taking us out to dinner."

"Have a great time," Jack said, lifting his hand in a wave. As he picked up the folders, he realized how valuable the woman had become to him and to the business in such a short time. He liked her no-nonsense attitude and her spunk, and he wanted to keep her around.

"Tuesday."

She turned back. "Yes?"

He reached into his pocket and removed a spare door key from his keyring, then tossed it to her. "You're hired."

She caught the key neatly, and a grin spread over her face. "Thank you, sir. I'll see you first thing in the morning." She fairly danced through the swinging doors and a few seconds later he heard the bell on the front door jangle as she left.

Jack turned back to his computer, whistling under his breath, realizing that by hiring an office manager, he'd made a commitment to grow their business. The idea of being spokesman for Tremont's was sinking in—the money would be good, and would allow him to put extra money into the business, to relieve some of the pressure for Derek. And as much as he hated to admit it, being the department store spokesman would still give him a thread of a connection with Alex.

When the bell on the door jangled again, Jack called, "Did you forget something?"

"Yeah," came Derek's voice. "I think I forgot our office address because I don't recognize this place."

Surprised, Jack jumped to his feet and hurried to the front, sporting a wide grin.

Looking tanned and happy, Derek and his new wife Janine stood in the front office, staring at the changes.

"You're home early," Jack said, pumping his brother's hand and lifting the blond Janine off her feet for a bear hug.

"Janine had to get back to see a doctor," Derek said, sliding an arm around her waist.

"Are you sick?" Jack asked, immediately concerned for his new sister.

"No." She beamed. "I'm pregnant!"

Elated, Jack clapped his brother on the back. "That didn't take long."

"Well," Derek said, a little sheepish, "we did have a long honeymoon."

"And a tiny head start," Janine said, holding up her thumb and forefinger.

"Shh," Derek chastised, but grinned anyway.

"Mother will have quite a surprise when she gets back," Jack said.

His brother nodded, then gestured to the office. "Speaking of surprises..."

"Oh, yeah," Jack said, "come on back and I'll show you around. The IRS auditor left this morning—we're in good shape—and Tuesday will be back first thing in the morning."

"Tuesday—you mean that woman who wandered in off the street?"

Jack dismissed his concern with a wave. "You'll love her."

Derek was impressed with the new furniture and equipment, but his first concern, of course, was cost.

"Already paid for," Jack assured him. "Compliments of Keeneland."

His brother laughed, shaking his head. When Janine excused herself to visit the restroom—Derek said she'd been doing a lot of that lately—his brother asked about the Tremont's account.

"The focus group results for the commercials came back today—we're in. Al Tremont wants us to meet next week to negotiate a long-term contract."

"That's great, Jack! Do you have some stills?"

Jack hesitated, then fished out the thick folder of photographs from the Tremont shoot and handed it to his brother.

Derek frowned. "These are all of you!"

"Sit down," Jack said, gesturing to a chair. He caught his brother up on the details of the spokesman-ad account tie-in as quickly as possible, leaving out the sordid details of his association with Alex.

Her brother squinted and scratched his head. "You're modeling now?"

Jack sighed. "It's not modeling."

"Well, whatever, it must have impressed the daughter."

Jack averted his gaze and nodded.

"What?" Derek asked.

"What do you mean, what?"

"That look."

"What look?"

"That I-got-a-woman-problem look."

Jack crossed his hands behind his head. "Not me, man."

Derek leaned forward in his chair and stared at Jack until he squirmed and cracked his knuckles in one sweeping motion. "You did it, didn't you?"

Jack frowned. "Did what?"

"Slept with her."

He stood and walked around to lean on the front of his desk, then sighed. "Okay, yeah."

His brother winced. "Ah, man! Tell me you didn't do it to get the business."

"Of course not!"

"So how will this affect your ability to work on the account? Does her father know?"

"He seems to know—"

"Christ, she *told* him?"

"I don't know, maybe she told her boyfriend, and *he* told her father."

Derek quirked an eyebrow. "Are the two men close?"

Jack cleared his throat. "Her boyfriend is the CFO."

"Oh, now *there's* a smooth move." Derek threw up his hands. "What were you thinking?"

Jack scowled. "That I could have this extremely pleasant conversation when you found out."

Derek shrugged. "Oh, well, if Tremont knows and he offered you the account anyway—"

"I won't be working directly with the daughter anymore." He picked up the minibasketball and tossed it toward the hoop. It bounced off the rim and rolled into a corner.

"And, um, how do you feel about that?"

Jack retrieved the ball and threw it up again. "When did

you become a shrink?'' The ball glanced off the rim again and bounced back to Derek.

"Since you became a case," his brother said, sending the ball swishing through the net. ''If I didn't know better, I'd say you were acting as if you were hung up on this woman.''

"And how am I acting?''

Derek crossed his arms and looked around the back office, taking in the new decor and the new computer equipment, the stack of completed paperwork on Jack's desk, and Jack's clothing—part of his Tremont's wardrobe. "Grown up.''

"Oh, very funny.''

"Enough, Jack," Derek said, his voice low and serious. ''Tell me about this woman.''

Jack dragged his hand down his face, willing to confess to murder if it would take away the nagging tightness in his chest. "Alex is...different.''

"Oh, hell.''

"Do you want to hear this or not?''

"Sorry, go ahead.''

He sighed, struggling to put into words the kinds of abstract things that had been floating through his mind like confetti. "Alex is...smart. And straight-laced. And she wears her hair in this tight little bun, except when she's on the bike with me...'' He groaned, realizing he sounded like a bad lyricist.

Derek laughed. "I don't believe it. My little brother has fallen in love.''

Jack jerked his head up. "Love? Whoa, I didn't say anything about love.''

"Who's in love?'' Janine asked, rejoining them.

Derek jerked his thumb toward Jack.

"Wait a minute!''

"Who is she?''

"His boss."

"That's not true!"

Janine grinned. "Is she in love with you, Jack?"

He frowned, objecting to the direction the conversation had taken. "I kind of doubt it, seeing how she's engaged to another man."

She slipped her arm around Derek's waist and gave him a squeeze. "Speaking from experience, sometimes a person doesn't realize they're settling until they meet the person they're really meant to love."

Out of respect, Jack didn't roll his eyes.

His brother winked. "You'd better let her know how you feel, Jack."

He scoffed. "Yeah, right."

"I know it sounds scary, but believe me, man, it's the not telling that'll eat you up." He smiled down at his wife and patted her stomach. "Ready to go home, sweetheart?"

She nodded, and they left, arm and arm, heads together, footsteps in synch. Jack watched, marveling at the change in his brother. He always thought his brother would settle down with a demure mouse, not a blond siren. But bubbly Janine had really brought out Derek's lighter side. In fact, they were complete opposites, just like—

On the other hand, lots of people were opposites, and it didn't mean they were in *love*.

Massaging the tightness just below his breastbone, Jack retrieved the basketball and spun it on the tip of his finger as his brother's and sister-in-law's words reverberated in his head. *You'd better let her know how you feel...it's the not telling that'll eat you up.*

But did he love her?

Jack eyed the basketball hoop and pursed his mouth. *L-O-V-E.* Four letters, four baskets. If he made them all, he might call, just to feel her up—er, out. And just to make it fair, he would close one eye and use his left hand.

He tossed the *L* ball.

Swish.

Dammit.

He tossed the *O* ball.

Swish.

Dammit.

He tossed the *V* ball.

Swish.

Dammit.

He tossed the *E* ball.

It rolled around the rim once, twice, three times...then popped out.

"Yeeesssss!" he shouted, pumping the air with his fist. He dropped back into his chair and waited for the relief to wash over him. Instead, his chest resumed its dull ache. He stared at the phone, then the clock. Four-thirty on Thursday afternoon. No doubt she was still at the office, possibly making plans to go out with Reddinger.

He could always call her and say it had been nice working with her, he reasoned, and picked up the phone.

But then she'd know that he knew about her losing the vice presidency. He put down the phone.

Then he brightened—calling to thank her for helping with the commercials would be simple and appropriate. He dialed her office number and drummed his fingers on his desk while the phone rang.

"Tess Hanover."

"This is Jack Stillman—"

"Oh, hellooooo, Mr. Stillman."

"Um, hello. I was trying to reach Alex. Is she available?"

"No," she said, her tone a little odd.

He frowned. "Has she left for the day?"

"You could say that."

Jack sighed. "Tess, did she or didn't she?"

"Actually," the woman said, her voice lowered to a conspiratorial level, "I shouldn't be telling you this, but Ms. Tremont resigned."

"*What?*"

"She and Mr. Reddinger both resigned," she whispered. "I heard that he got a great job offer in Cincinnati."

And Alex was going with him. Jack's heart sank.

"Ms. Tremont and her father had an argument."

He hated to snoop, but the woman seemed anxious to tell him something. "What about?"

"Mr. Tremont barged into her office, and I overheard him blame her for nearly losing you as a spokesman."

Jack swallowed hard. "What did he say?"

"That she'd gone back on her promise to try to work with you, and the reason you had changed your mind was because she was so difficult to get along with."

He closed his eyes. "That's not true."

"He sounded angry. Ms. Tremont offered to step aside and let someone else work with you, but he told her the new vice president would be taking over those responsibilities." Relishing every detail, Tess's voice rolled with inflection. "Then a little while later, Mr. Reddinger arrived and went into Ms. Tremont's office. They came out together and asked me to make official copies of their resignation letters."

He felt as if he'd been punched in the gut. "Is Al still there?"

"Yes."

"Patch me through to him, please." Feeling as if Alex were slipping through his fingers, he stood and paced until Al Tremont's voice came on the line.

"Jack, what's up?"

He wasted no time on formalities. "What's this about you telling Alex I couldn't work with her because she was too difficult to get along with?"

"Well, that's what you said, Jack."

"No, I said I couldn't work with Alex, but I didn't tell you why. We both jumped to conclusions about what the other person meant."

"I'm confused, son. Why can't you work with Alex?"

Sweat broke out on his upper lip, and the pain in his chest escalated to the point of forcing him to sit down.

"Jack?"

"I love her." He leaned his head back, waiting for the fall-out.

"What?" Al sounded incredulous.

"I love your daughter."

The man made a few blustery sounds. "Does Alex know?"

"Not unless she's a mind reader."

"Well, son, you'd better get a move on."

"I understand she and Reddinger both resigned."

Al made a rueful sound. "I can replace Heath, but not Alex. I can't believe she's leaving for *him*."

"Maybe she's leaving because she feels unappreciated at Tremont's," Jack ventured.

"Why, that's absurd."

"Is it? I know she was hoping for that vice presidency."

"Jack, just between you and me, I was planning to step down in the next couple of months, and recommend that Alex take over as president. *That's* why she didn't get the vice presidency."

Shocked, Jack asked, "Why didn't you tell her?"

"When she told me she was leaving with Reddinger, I didn't want to muddy the waters. You see, son, I'm more concerned that Alex be with the right man than that she take over the family business." Al laughed with no humor. "I guess neither one of us has been as forthcoming with Alex as we should have been. But I'll make you a deal. If you can talk her into staying in Lexington, I'll offer her the presidency." Al made a regretful noise. "Jack...if you can keep my daughter from leaving me, I would be in your debt."

Jack swallowed. "Maybe you should offer her the presidency first, just to sweeten the deal."

"Sorry, son, I don't want to get in the way here. You're on your own."

18

"DID HE TAKE IT HARD?" Lana asked, licking mocha cocoa cake icing from a silver spoon.

"Who, Daddy or Heath?" Alex sucked down fantasy fudge.

Lana leaned against the couch arm. "Both."

She heaved a sigh, her head still spinning from the day's events. "Daddy didn't make a fuss, said he was disappointed I was leaving Tremont's, but wanted me to be happy." Alex shook her head. "After all these years, he has no idea how much he and the company mean to me. I'm going to be more diligent about spending time with Daddy—even if it means putting up with Gloria—but it's time I move on in my career."

"And Heath?"

She wrinkled her nose. "I think he was more bothered by the thought of living alone in a new city than by the thought of losing me."

"What are you going to do now?"

Alex shrugged. "I don't know. Maybe you and I can buy a coffee shop."

Lana pointed her spoon. "I was talking about Jack."

Her heart clenched. "What does Jack have to do with all this?"

"*Please*. Only that you're in love with the man."

She scraped her spoon against the bottom to get the last trace of chocolate, but it was hard to see through the film of tears. "So is every other woman in the city. If Jack Stillman were open for business, I'd have to take a number to be served."

"Not true. He has a thing for you."

Shaking her head, Alex tried to smile. "Yeah, he called it a 'friendly curiosity.' Besides, he told my father he couldn't work with me, so what does that tell you?"

Ping.

Alex dropped her spoon and jerked her head toward the sliding glass door.

"What's that?" Lana asked.

Ping.

Her heart lifted, tentatively. "Excuse me." She walked to the glass door and opened it in time to take a hit on the top of her head. "Ow!" Crouching low, she made her way to the rail, then leaned over, frowning. "You almost gave me a concussion!"

Jack stopped, then dropped a handful of pebbles next to his bike parked in the grass. He tilted his head back and offered up a tentative grin. "Women with concussions are much easier to persuade."

Refusing to get her hopes up, Alex crossed her arms. "Persuade to do what?"

"To not go to Cincinnati with Reddinger."

Behind her, Lana gasped, but Alex would only allow herself the smallest thrill. "And do what instead?"

He hesitated so long, she thought he wasn't going to respond. "Stay...stay here with me."

Behind her, Lana whimpered, but Alex still had a bone to pick with Jack. "Why would you want me to stay, when I'm so difficult to get along with that you can't even work with me?"

His shoulders fell. "Your father misunderstood. When I said that I couldn't work with you, I meant I couldn't because..."

"Because why? I didn't hear you."

"Because I love you!"

Behind her, Lana cried out and, at last, Alex allowed her heart to soar. Still, she tried to remain nonchalant. "I'm not sure if I believe you."

He scratched his temple. "I figured as much." Then he turned to his bike and unstrapped a large box. "Okay, I'm coming up."

She watched with delighted disbelief as he marched across the grass beneath the balcony.

"What's he doing?" Lana whispered.

"He's climbing up the fire escape," Alex whispered back. "Scram!"

"No way. I want to see this."

"*Goodbye*, Lana."

"Oh, all right. Call me, would you?"

"Sure."

She thought her heart might come out of her chest. Was it possible? Did this man love her? Slowly he hauled himself and the box up the fire escape ladder. Alex held her breath until his smiling face appeared on the other side of her balcony railing.

His eyes were serious, his expression earnest. "Alex, I don't have anything to offer you except my heart and my devotion, but I want to try to make you happy." He glanced at her hand, then frowned. "Where's your engagement ring?"

"I returned it," she said, feeling herself misting up.

"Why?" he asked, his dark eyes hopeful.

"Because I love you," she whispered.

A grin split his handsome face, then he pulled her mouth to his for a deep, promising kiss.

Suddenly Alex pulled back. "I'm unemployed now."

Jack shook his head. "I don't think so, Madam President."

She frowned. "What?"

"Your father has news. We'll call him," he said simply, then nipped at her neck, "afterward."

Alex tilted her head back, reveling in the thrill of his mouth, his tongue, his teeth on her skin. "Yes, afterward," she murmured. "Are you coming over?"

He lifted his head, as if he'd just remembered he was suspended three stories up. "Absolutely."

"Jack, what's in the box?"

His grin was sheepish. "Um, I bought you a hat," he said, handing her the box, then climbed over the rail to join her. "One that I thought would suit you."

"Can I open it?"

He swallowed, then exhaled noisily, as if gathering his strength. "Go ahead."

Alex bit her bottom lip and lifted the lid, then sucked in a sharp breath.

On a cloud of netting sat a white bridal hat, with a short, pearl-studded veil.

"Oh...oh...oh." Happy tears streamed down her face as she kissed him.

"My brother convinced me that love like this doesn't come around but once in a lifetime," he said. "But before I get down on one knee, I have a confession to make."

Alex swallowed, her joy suspended for a second. "What?"

He winced. "Remember the day you showed up at my office?"

She nodded. How could she forget?

"I wasn't setting you up for my ad pitch. I thought you were an IRS agent, and what you saw was the way the agency and I really were—a complete mess."

She stuck her tongue in her cheek to suppress her mirth. "So what happened?"

He splayed his hands. "What can I say? You made me

want to straighten up my act, and it feels...right. *We* feel right, Alex."

Incredibly touched, Alex cleared her throat. "You were about to get down on one knee?"

He grinned and swooped down in obvious relief. "Alex, will you marry me?"

"But I thought you were against marriage...I thought you said—"

"My knees aren't what they used to be, sweetheart. Is that a yes or a no?"

Alex laughed. "Yes."

His face split into a grin, then he shot to his feet and swung her around, whooping. At last he set her on her feet, then situated the little white hat on her head and kissed her until she was breathless. Warm and alight with his love, Alex finally pulled away, laughing. "Wait...I have to...call Lana."

But Jack shook his head, then leaned over to scoop her into his arms and carry her into the loft. "Afterward."

─── Epilogue ───

"ALEX," LANA SAID from the doorway of the dressing room. "Can your father come in?"

Alex tucked an errant strand of hair beneath the bridal hat Jack had given her and smiled at her maid of honor from the dressing vanity. "Yes, Lana, please send him in."

She stood and smoothed the skirt of her gown, simple white silk. Her heart thumped with elation and anticipation. Over the past few months, she and Jack had grown closer every day, their love deepening as their friendship and passion bloomed. She felt very special and extremely blessed to be marrying such a wonderful man.

"If only your mother could see you."

Alex turned to see her father standing just inside the dressing room, splendidly handsome in his tuxedo, beaming.

"She would be so proud," he murmured, his voice catching.

She walked toward him slowly. "But what do *you* think, Daddy?"

He met her in the middle of the room and she was astonished to see his eyes were moist. "I think," he said, his voice throaty, "that I am the luckiest man on this earth to have such an amazing, beautiful, talented woman for my daughter."

Her eyes filled with tears as she lifted her arms to hug his neck, counting yet another blessing—she and her father had grown as close as she'd always hoped. And Alex had even begun to forge a tentative relationship with Gloria.

Her father smiled down at her and stroked her cheek with his thumb. "And I'd say that Jack is the second luckiest man on this earth."

Alex straightened his bow tie. "Thank you, Daddy. And in Jack you're finally getting a son."

Her father's blue eyes turned questioning. "What do you mean?"

She gave him a small smile. "A son, Daddy, like you've always wanted."

A strange expression came over his face. "I couldn't be happier that you and Jack are making a life together, Alex, but whatever gave you the idea that I wanted a son?"

Alex balked. "Well...you're so into sports...and you get along so well with Jack...and I always thought..."

His laugh rumbled out, low and rueful, then he took both her hands in his. "Alex, my dear heart, I would've been glad for any more children your mother and I might have had, but when she first told me she was pregnant, I never imagined having anything *but* a beautiful little girl to love and who would love me in return. I'm sorry if I ever gave you the impression that you weren't *everything* I'd dreamed of in a child. Alex, I love you more than life itself and I'm so proud of you, I'm...speechless."

Her eyes overflowed as she wrapped her arms around his middle. "Daddy, thank you, thank you."

"Hey, you two," Lana said from the doorway. "We're waiting."

They separated, and Alex wiped at her tears.

"Are you ready, my dear?" her father asked.

She nodded, sniffing her tears dry. She claimed her bouquet, then smiled at her father as he lowered the short veil over her face.

"My last walk with my little girl," he said, extending his arm.

She took his arm, blinking rapidly. "I'll always be your little girl, Daddy."

"Jack's probably wondering if I'm going to keep you," he said gruffly. "We'd better get going."

By the time they reached the doorway of the chapel, Alex had composed herself enough that she could clearly see Jack, stunning in his tuxedo, waiting for her at the altar, his brother Derek by his side. When Jack's face lit up, her heart nearly burst with happiness. Her father squeezed her arm and she began to walk toward Jack, her friend, her lover, her soul mate.

"Happy, sweetheart?" her father whispered.

"How could I not be, Daddy?" she said, squeezing back. "I have the two most wonderful men in the world to love."

For those of you who enjoyed

IT TAKES A REBEL,

here's a sneak peak
at Stephanie Bond's next book...

#787 TOO HOT TO SLEEP

Temptation Blaze
on sale June 2000

GEORGIA ADAMS DECIDED that her friend was right on one score—Georgia's lackluster boyfriend Rob *was* waiting for her to make a move. And so she had settled upon the least threatening and most erotic option that had crossed her mind to fix that situation: phone sex. The fact that she'd never participated in phone sex before only heightened her anticipation. After all, how hard could it be?

She sat on the edge of the bed and glanced at the clock. One-thirty a.m.—Rob would be deep asleep, but if her hunch was right, he'd be wide awake within a few seconds. Before she had time to reconsider, she picked up the phone and pushed the "zero," then the "one" button to retrieve Rob's pre-programmed number.

After the third ring, his sleep-fuzzy voice came over the line. "Hello?"

Her heart thudded so loudly she could barely hear him. "Hello, Rob, this is Georgia."

"Hmm?"

"D-don't talk," she said. Then she leaned back against a pile of pillows and lowered her voice to what she hoped was a sexy tone. "Just listen."

OFFICER KEN MEDLOCK should have been used to late-night calls, but he still had trouble focusing on the voice at the other end of the line. Did the woman say she was "Georgia"? His mind spun as he tried to place the name—a new dispatcher?

"I know it's late, but I've been thinking about...us...all evening and I was wondering...that is..." The woman with the sultry voice inhaled and Ken opened his mouth to tell her she had the wrong number.

"I'm not wearing panties."

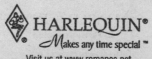

HEART OF THE WEST

Every Man Has His Price!

Lost Springs Ranch was
famous for turning young
mavericks into good men.
So word that the ranch was
in financial trouble sent
a herd of loyal bachelors
stampeding back to
Wyoming to put themselves
on the auction block!

HARLEQUIN®
Makes any time special ™

Visit us at www.romance.net

PHHOWGEN